EB

Duel at Cheyenne

George Willowfield learned a long time ago that in life everything had to be paid for. You paid in money, blood, or sweat or time, but you paid.

For George, the easiest way was money. So he stole a train and asked the US government for $250,000 to get it back.

That's when Frank Angel stepped in – to deliver the ransom and trail the guy who collected it – until he got the money or the guy. The government doesn't like to be held up and Frank was there to see the debt paid – one way or another!

Duel at Cheyenne

Daniel Rockfern

A Black Horse Western

ROBERT HALE · LONDON

© Frederick Nolan, 1975, 2008
First hardcover edition 2008
Originally published in paperback as *Duel at Cheyenne*
by Frederick H. Christian

ISBN 978-0-7090-7687-2

Robert Hale Limited
Clerkenwell House
Clerkenwell Green
London EC1R 0HT

www.halebooks.com

Typeset by
Derek Doyle & Associates, Shaw Heath
Printed and bound in Great Britain by
Antony Rowe Limited, Wiltshire

ONE

As soon as he saw the train, the lookout gave the signal. She came around the bend past his hiding place and went into the cut like some great prehistoric beast, roaring, clanking, her carriages swaying, smoke bellowing as the two locomotives put their backs into taking her up the gradient of Sweetwater Cut. She was a big train, and very special, with those two gaudy UP locos up front. Heading her up was Engine Number 47, 'Grizzly Bear' – one of Matthias Baldwin's 4-4-0s – but Number 47, impressive though she was, couldn't begin to compare with the huge ten-wheel 'White Fox' behind her. Great gleaming reflector lamps above her cow-catcher, bright brasswork shining all around the cabin with its comfortably padded driving seats, 'White Fox' was one of the showpieces of the Union Pacific stable and nobody was more proud of her than her engineer, Patrick Grady. Inside the cabin, he gave the Fox a quarter-turn more throttle, then leaned out of his window and checked back along the length of the train.

Immediately behind his tender, Grady could see the 45-foot express car, with the armed guards on the platform at both ends, riot guns slung from their shoulders on leather loops. Behind the express car were two ornate Silver

Palace Pullman carriages, each of them a good sixty feet long; and behind these was a smoking car equally as long. Five ordinary – at least from the outside – passenger coaches made up the rest of the train's length. She took the best part of ten minutes to pass the hiding place of the lookout on the bluff above the entrance to the Cut. He watched her go up the slight incline with the furling smoke laid back across the tops of the carriages like a fur collar. He smiled – not with pleasure – and gave the second signal.

Engineer Pat Grady nodded as he pulled his head inside the cabin: all well. He laid his gnarled hand on the whistle cord and gave it a long, considered pull, grinning as the sudden screech of the whistle bounced off the rocky face of the cut alongside the train and startled wood pigeons burst out of the trees below in a panicking blur of gray and white. He fished his big gold turnip watch out of a vest pocket – a presentation from the president of the Union Pacific Railroad himself – and checked the time: 2:33. On time, he thought with satisfaction. It was a matter of pride with him, and indeed every engineer on the road, to keep to the schedule no matter what. Grady was an old sweat. He'd been with UP since the beginning, starting as a wiper swabbing caked oil from the engines back in the roundhouse in Kansas City, working his way up the ladder to the lofty position of engineer, perversely proud of being half-homeless (a man never knew on Monday where he'd be sleeping on Wednesday night, they used to say). One of his most valued possessions was a photograph of the driving of the Golden Spike at Promontory Point, the day the UP and the CP lines had met to complete the transcontinental railroad – May 10, 1869 – and the president of the UP, Leland Stanford, there to drive the last spike. Even if he'd missed the first time, it was a wonderful day. Grady had found himself a good spot on the side of Engine Number 119 just abaft the smokestack, and he'd stood there in his high boots, his flat peaked cap at a jaunty angle and his hand on his hip to keep him steady while the photographer shouted out the long seconds. Everyone always said what a fine portrait of him it was. It was such a career that finally brought a man like Grady to where he was now: being in charge of this Special was the most important job he'd ever had or was ever likely to have. And he meant to see that there were no slip-ups, none at all. He slid a sideways glance at his fireman, Harry Owney, a thick-set, red-faced, long-armed man, whose very expression proclaimed the nationality that was evident in his brogue when he spoke.

'Right on time,' Grady shouted above the engine noise. Owney nodded.

'We'll be in Cheyenne by four,' he observed.

'Aye,' Grady said, nodding as though pleased – which he was. They would make Cheyenne, Wyoming, comfortably by four in the afternoon, right on schedule. He was looking forward to the welcome they would receive, as they had been welcomed in other towns and cities across the country: after all, this was no ordinary train. He wondered if they had a brass band in Cheyenne. Very fond of a bit of brass band music, Grady was.

'I wonder if they'll have a brass band, then?' he shouted to Owney.

'Sure and they ought to,' Owney yelled back. 'At the very least.'

Right, Grady thought, they should indeed, for such a train as the Freedom Train was so out of the ordinary as to beggar comparisons. She wasn't just a Special, she was

7

unique, the Special of Specials, the once-in-a-lifetime train. Every man on the crew – engineers, firemen, brakemen, and conductor (although there wasn't a man aboard with a ticket for him to punch) – had fought, competed for the honor of being aboard. She was the Freedom Train and she was worth a hundred million dollars, if there was such a thing as a price for the cargo she carried.

America had planned two enormous, spectacular events to mark this year of 1876, the centennial of her independence. One of the projects was the Centennial Exposition in Philadelphia's Fairmount Park, opened the preceding May by President Ulysses S. Grant. It was planned to be, and had become, the largest, most spectacular, most successful exposition ever staged anywhere in the entire world. It was said that by the time the exposition closed on November 10, about a month from now, nearly ten million people would have paid to see it, which wasn't too bad for a country whose total population wasn't much over forty million.

The second project was the Freedom Train thundering now through the Sweetwater Cut en route to Cheyenne, Wyoming. It was one more stop in a whole roster of stops which had taken the Freedom Train all over the country as part of a tour of ten thousand miles and more. It stretched from Seattle and Portland to San Francisco and Sacramento and from there to Salt Lake City and Denver and Fort Worth – all across the length and breadth of these United States. She had set out in April, and now, as the nights of early October drew in, she was on the homeward run toward Kansas City and Omaha and St. Louis. The Freedom Train was an inspired idea, and it had enabled many hundreds of thousands of people who would otherwise never have had the chance to share in the celebration of the centennial by seeing an exhibition of the republic's most treasured artifacts. Packed carefully in specially constructed crates in the express car, under the frowning guard of a dozen hand-picked honor cadets from the Military Academy of West Point, was a complete exhibition of one hundred years of American history.

At each of the scheduled stops along the route, the whole train became a walk-through exhibition. The passenger cars and the Pullman carriages had been gutted and then refitted especially for this purpose.

The rearmost passenger carriage and the caboose served as quarters and dormitory for the soldier boys, as Grady called them (to their infinite disgust). At the end of each layover, the cadets would lend a hand as the two experts from the Smithsonian Institution, who were aboard to answer questions from the public and to care-take the exhibits, dismantled the exhibition and packed everything carefully into the velvet-lined packing cases. Then the express car would be locked and shuttered from the inside and the guards posted on the platforms at both ends. Grady and Pat O'Connor, the engineer on Number 47, would get up steam and move her out to her next destination.

The Freedom Train was a brainchild of the president's Special Committee for the Celebration of the Centennial – a clutch of formidable old biddies whose main qualification for the job was that they were either the wives of prominent members of the Republican administration or Washington freeloaders to whom Grant owed a favor. They had had at least four hundred ideas, but this was the only good one. It had quickly been recognized as such, and the idea – to send out America's history for the people to see – had reached fruition very quickly. Thus it came about that rocking gently in their special containers in the express car were the original Declaration of Independence drafted by Thomas Jefferson; George Washington's own copy of the Constitution; a holographic copy of the four-stanza poem by Francis Scott Key, which had been written following the bombardment of Fort McHenry, *The Star Spangled Banner*; a montage of flags that illustrated the development of the national flag; the glass-cased pillow, stained with the President's blood, which had been on the bed in the Petersen house in Washington where Lincoln had died; the original manuscript of Mrs Beecher Stowe's famous novel *Uncle Tom's Cabin*; Robert E. Lee's sword, surrendered to Grant at Appomattox Courthouse; the bill of sale for the Louisiana Purchase of 1803; the tattered flag from the Alamo; the first clock made in the United States (Eli Terry, 1800); and much, much more: early revolvers; Whitney's drawings for the cotton gin; Fulton's 1807 designs for the paddlesteamer *Clermont*; Linus Yale's cylinder lock; Gliddon's typewriting machine; the first Bible printed in America; a letter in Lincoln's handwriting to Grace Bedell dated October 19, 1860. The organizers had done everything they could to present all the aspects of the country's history, while avoiding areas which might arouse contention or dispute. The estimated value of the contents of the train – estimated because no insurance company in the world, not even Lloyds of London, would go so far as to commit itself to an appraisal of the worth of these priceless, irreplaceable artifacts – was one hundred million dollars. But money could never substitute for the loss of such treasures. Not, for a moment, that anyone expected that.

Engineer Grady eased on his brake at the crest of the gradient, ready to hold the huge train on the downhill run to Cheyenne. He leaned out of the cabin to flag O'Connor a signal to do the same thing, and as he did, Willowfield sprung his trap.

Gil Curtis had planted dynamite carefully in the rock walls of the Sweetwater Cut at two marks about half a mile apart. They went off now with a cracking boom and Grady, quite instinctively, grabbed at the huge brake lever, throwing his full weight against it as he saw the rock wall of the Cut ahead bulge out, lean over, as if in some strange slow, arrested motion, then roar down on to the track perhaps three hundred yards ahead of the train.

The locked wheels gouged into the metal tracks, making huge showers of sparks which arced outward from beneath the locomotive as it yawed and screeched and rocked and squealed, slowing and shuddering slower until it came to a panting halt not fifty yards away from where the clattering pile of boulders, with its corona of sifting rock dust, lay like a manmade mountain across the right of way. Before they even had a chance to regain their balance properly, before the train had come to a final steaming stop, Willowfield's men had shot the two guards off the platforms of the express car.

'What in the name of all the saints is goin' on out there?' roared Grady. He swung down from his cabin on to the oily graveled right of way and glared up at the lip of the defile above him as if it had personally insulted him. His gaze shuttled toward the sprawled figures of the dead guards and then up in puzzlement at Owney, who had come to the footstep of the engine, eyes searching up, down, right, left, fear in them. Down behind them, dust rose against the clear sky. The dull boom of the twin explosions seemed still to be reverberating against the walls of the cutting. The dead guards looked like discarded dolls.

11

Nothing moved anywhere.

Two of the West Point cadets were coming nervously out of the express car, Springfield bolt-action rifles ported across their bodies in the regulation manner, scanning the lip of the defile with frightened determination.

'Get back there!' Grady yelled. 'Get back inside! Can't you see it's a—'

He never got the word 'holdup' out. A fusillade of rifle shots thundered out from the lip of the defile, and Grady was spun off his feet by the ambushers' bullets, dead before he stopped rolling down the banked incline alongside the right of way. The two cadets who had emerged from the express car recoiled in panic, scrambling for the safety of the steel-lined doorway. One of them made it. The other threw up his hands as if in despair as someone on the rim shot the top of his head off. The Springfield rifle made a tinny scrabble on the gravel as it slid down beside his body, and then there was an enormous silence, broken only by the hiss of escaping steam beneath the big woodburners and the steady monotone of Harry Owney's curses from the dubious safety of the cabin of his locomotive.

The cadets in the express car slammed the doors, bolting and barring them, taking their positions alongside the specially constructed steel flaps through which they, like the archers in medieval castles, had a field of vision through a vertical slot with fluted sides on the inside. They looked at the young officer standing in the center of the express car, sweat beading his upper lip, awaiting his orders.

Outside, nothing moved that anyone on the train could see. Willowfield sent just one man down, one man who sneaked up to the rear of the train and wormed beneath it, working his way on hands and knees over the oily ties, dragging a canvas bag. When he reached the express car he withdrew bundled sticks of dynamite from the bag, and then carefully and precisely wired them first to the front wheel bogy and then to the rear. Each bundle was of eight sticks, and he used three bundles for each bogy. Then he attached the detonator caps and wires, and wormed back down the length of the train, paying out wire behind him like a silkworm. When he reached the end of the train he slid down the incline and ran for the rim above where the end of the wire connected to the plunger was lying. Connecting them quickly, he stood clear and gave his signal.

Up on the rim, Willowfield acknowledged the signal.

He nodded with satisfaction; everything was going according to plan. He was a man of no more than medium height but he was gross, jowly, clumsy, bathed in sweat as the glancing sun boiled off the gargantuan rocks around him. He weighed almost three hundred pounds, but nobody who had ever had any truck with him would have said that he was soft. Just one look into his reptilian eyes, eyes which hardly ever blinked, would have immediately dispelled any such notion. His mouth was like a knife wound, his nose as imperious and hooked as that of any Roman emperor. He looked like what he was, a degenerate voluptuary who would sacrifice any man or anything on the altar of his own ambitions.

'You down there!' he shouted from the edge of the cut. His voice was harsh and impatient because he made it so. Normally he spoke very softly. He believed you caught more flies with honey than with vinegar.

'You down there!' he yelled again. 'Do you hear me?' His voice bounced off the rocky walls of the Sweetwater

Cut, echoing into infinity. A buzzard flapped squawking in panic out of the pines below.

In the express car, Captain Benedict Nicolson looked at the cadets standing to at their loopholes, waiting for his command, waiting for his reaction to Willowfield's shout. They were all staring at him and he did not know what to do. He could feel sweat trickling down his body underneath the tailored uniform. He felt tricked, betrayed. After all, this was supposed to have been an honor guard, not a combat unit. He had been specially selected, and so had the cadets, not for military duty, but for smartness, education, for – well, admit it, for *class*. There had been no indication that anything like this was going to happen and it wasn't fair. They had promised him a minor decoration at the conclusion of the tour. Now. . . ? Master Sergeant Alex Wells looked at the young officer and grimaced. As was always the case, the army had sent boys on men's work. This young captain, now: he looks as if he was going to wet his beautifully cut infantry grays any moment, while these boy-soldiers probably already have. Still, he thought, 'tis not the captain's fault he's the son-in-law of the brigadier commanding the adjutant-general's department in Chicago. Nor could you blame him for grabbing a featherbed number like the Freedom Train, seeing the country at the country's expense. After all, wasn't every man on the train doing the same? Not a one of them a fighting man, himself – alas – now included. It was a dozen years since he'd heard the buzz of bullets at Gettysburg, and a dozen years was a long time between fights. These boy-soldiers, now: they could probably load and aim those Springfields they were holding on to so grimly, but whether in a real fight they'd be able to do much more than use up ammunition he wouldn't want to say. Commanded as they were

by this whey-faced popinjay who'd obviously never heard a
shot fired in anger, he didn't rate their chances highly at
all. None of what he was thinking showed on his face when
he spoke.

'Sir,' he said, prompting Nicolson. 'Sir?'

'Yes,' said the captain. 'Yes.' Then, as if waking from a
reverie, he drew himself erect. 'Tell them we hear them,
Master Sa'rnt,' he said crisply. 'Ask them—'

Wells was already elbowing one of the cadets away from
the slot nearest him. Putting his mouth to the aperture, he
pulled in a deep breath and then bellowed 'You up there!'

'We hear you!' came the reply.

'Who are you?' Wells shouted. 'What do you want?'

Willowfield told them.

He told them that he had a hundred men behind him,
which was a considerable exaggeration they were in no
position to challenge. He told them he was giving them a
five-minute truce in which to send a man to check his
statement that there was enough dynamite beneath the
express car to blow it the rest of the way to Cheyenne.
After that, he told them, they had two more minutes in
which to throw their weapons out of the express car, and
come out with their hands on their heads. Then he waited
while Master-Sergeant Wells swung down from the express
car, ducked beneath it, and returned to report his findings
to Captain Nicolson.

'It,' Captain Nicolson said. 'He. It can't be. True, I
mean. He couldn't. Won't. Sergeant, you don't think he'd
blow the train up do you?'

He was thinking of the priceless treasures which were,
at least nominally, his responsibility, and about what their
loss would mean to his career. These bandits obviously
intended to steal them. There was little choice: he must

die heroically defending them. He drew himself erect again.

'I'll go out there,' he said, pulling his tunic down. 'I'll talk—'

'Begging the captain's pardon,' Sergeant Wells said, sharply. He knew better than to actually lay a hand on the officer, but he also knew that if he had to, he'd knock the silly bastard unconscious before he let him step outside the car.

'Meaning no disrespect, sir,' he said quickly as Nicolson paused. 'But those bas – those people out there have already killed three men. We'll prove nothing by letting them have you for a target.'

Nicolson blanched. It hadn't occurred to him that they would quite likely kill him out of hand.

He probably thinks they wouldn't dare, Wells thought, him being the brigadier's son.

'Well,' Nicolson said, as though considering every aspect of what Wells had just said. 'Well, then. I think we may just let them sweat it out.'

'Sir?' Wells said, aghast. What was the stupid bastard up to now?

'Sergeant,' Nicolson said, patiently, using the tone that a grownup uses to explain a concept to a small child. 'They want what is in this baggage car. They cannot get it with us in here.'

'Sir,' Wells said, carefully. 'The dynamite. . . .'

'They'd never set it off,' Nicolson said, confidently. 'Destroying the contents of the express car would negate the purpose of the holdup.'

He looked defiantly at the cadets. Not one of them would meet his eye. He was about to open his mouth again when Willowfield shouted once more.

'You have exactly one minute left!' he yelled.

Nicolson heard the words and broke like a reed. 'Oh, my God,' he groaned. 'Sergeant. . . .'

Master-Sergeant Wells was already wrestling with the bolts of the express car door.

By the time Willowfield came down from the rim with five heavily armed men to back him up, the cadets were on the track, their weapons at their feet, hands on their heads. Willowfield surveyed them with satisfaction, and their officer with undisguised contempt. Leaving them to stand beneath the cold regard of his men, he climbed awkwardly into the express car, and surveyed the contents with a small smile playing on his face. No triumph: not yet. There was still a very great deal to do. Yet he was strangely elated. George Willowfield, he thought, you have come a long way. A long way from the parade ground at Salisbury where they had drummed him out of the Queen's Own 17th Lancers, a long way from the canebreaks of Missouri where he'd ridden on the coat-tails of Quantrill's cutthroats. What he had done here today would make Jesse and Frank James look like the country louts they had always been. George Willowfield had done the impossible.

The Freedom Train was his.

TWO

'You're sure it's not a hoax.'

It wasn't really a question, and the speaker, a gray-haired man in his mid-fifties, didn't really expect an answer. Nevertheless, President Ulysses S. Grant gave him one.

'It's not a hoax,' he said.

The two of them were sitting on opposite sides of the president's rosewood desk in the Oval Office of the Executive Mansion. Through the window across the porch the rose garden was still bright with nodding blooms and the scent of late magnolia blossom came through the open windows. At this time of year, squirrels would come down from the trees and eat from your hand in the gardens. Grant looked drawn and tired, as well he might, the visitor thought. 1876 had been a pretty bad year for the president. Nobody had actually gone as far as to accuse Grant of venery, but there'd been enough hinting to sink a battleship. The Belknap scandal, the destruction of the 7th Cavalry at Little Big Horn, everything from malfeasance to vote-rigging had been laid at Grant's door, and there was no question that in the forthcoming election he would leave the Executive Mansion forever. And if U.S. (Unconditional Surrender) Grant's year had been nothing but bad news so far, the holdup of the Freedom Train was just about the right weight of straw to break the camel's back. 'You've read the letter,' the president said.

'I have indeed.'

'And?'

'And I think we'd better make arrangements to get the money together.'

'You'd pay?'

'There is no option, Mr President. We have to play for time.'

'Time,' the president said, rolling the word around his mouth as if he were tasting it. I could do with a little of that myself, he thought. He leaned back in the big brass-studded leather armchair and relit his cigar, waving at the humidor on his desk by way of invitation.

'No, thank you,' the attorney general said. 'I'll smoke my own.'

He picked up the letter and read it for perhaps the twentieth time, thinking how fast this situation had developed, snowballed. The nonarrival of the Freedom Train at Cheyenne. The discovery, almost immediately, that the telegraph lines between that place and Laramie – from where the Freedom Train was due – were dead. Then, before the UP officials at Cheyenne had put together a special train to go up the track to look for the missing train, Engineer Pat O'Connor had arrived on a lathered horse and given his account of the fate of the Freedom Train. That information, together with the text of the letter which the attorney general now held in his hand, had been telegraphed instantly to Washington.

General U.S. Grant, President of the United States.

Sir,

My men and I have captured the Freedom Train. We are holding it presently at Sweetwater Cut, Wyoming Territory, where both its personnel and its contents remain safe. The price of its release is $250,000. This sum, in used currency of denominations no larger than fifty dollars, is to be sent to a destination I shall designate upon receipt of your agreement to my terms, which should be forthcoming no later than 48 hours after your receipt of this message. If I have received no such agreement by midnight, Tuesday, October 3, the Freedom Train and its contents will be destroyed and all its personnel executed. Lest you be misguided enough to consider armed action of any kind in relief of the train, I would advise you to first consult the Army Topographical Corps for details of the configurations of the Sweetwater Cut and the impossibility of attacking it in any way which would preclude my executing the destruction of the train. The army map grid-references are Sheet 154A/2 North 1422/ West 45. 1 enclose a bona-fide.

> *Your obedient servant,*
> *George Willowfield.*

'What was the bona-fide?' the attorney general asked.

Grant gestured at the sheet of paper in a sandwich between two pieces of glass which lay upon his desk: the flowery script plainly gave the title of the poem,

The Star Spangled Banner.

'Someone from the Library of Congress is coming to pick it up later,' Grant grunted.

'Ah, yes,' smiled his visitor. 'I imagine they would.'

Grant leaned forward in his chair now, his brow knotted in anger, using his cigar in jabbing emphasis of his points.

'I won't have it, Charles!' he growled. 'It's not on. I won't have some goddamned renegade holding the United States of America to ransom!'

The attorney general said nothing.

'Oh, I know what you're thinking,' Grant said. 'You think I'm worried about my reputation, more mud to throw at the Party just before the election. It's not that, I assure you. There's a principle involved. I'd rather order the entire goddamned army into the field than knuckle under to this . . . this scum, whoever he is. Send them out and tell them to take him and hang him to the nearest goddamned tree they can find!'

'I know how you must feel, Mr President,' the attorney general said, 'but we don't dare use force. If he actually carried out his threat to destroy the train . . . Did you speak with the Topographical Corps?'

'Yes, dammit!' snarled Grant, slapping the desk in his impatience. 'They confirmed what this, this Willowfield claims. No way of even getting close to that damned train without being spotted. Two men could hold Sweetwater Cut against a hundred.'

'Yes,' the attorney general said. 'This Willowfield gives every indication of having planned his raid down to the smallest detail. I think we must send word that we accept.'

Grant looked up, his expression mule-stubborn. His gaze locked with the level eyes of the attorney general and then dropped. The angry light in his eyes faded and he shrugged, pressing a bell on his desk top. The double doors opened and one of his aides came in.

'Get a clear line through to the United States marshal

in Cheyenne, Wyoming Territory,' Grant said, speaking
slowly, as if every word was being dragged out of him with
pincers. He scribbled something on a notepad, tore the
page off and handed it to the man. 'Send this.'

'Yes, sir,' the aide said, taking the paper and leaving the
room, already on the run. The news of the ransom of the
Freedom Train was already the hottest topic inside the
Executive Mansion, and bets were being laid on what
Grant would do. The aide read the scrawled words and
shook his head.

'Advise Willowfield of my acceptance,' he said aloud.
'Inform me immediately of his reply.'

Well, he thought, the president had better know what
he was doing. Just handing over a quarter of a million
dollars to some gang of renegades out west was very
dangerous ground for anyone in Government. For the
president of the United States to do it was suicidal. There
wasn't a damned thing in Article Two that gave him that
kind of freedom. The in-joke around the place was that
Grant was hoping the renegades would burn the
Constitution, so that he could write a new one himself
which covered his actions. The aide hurried down the hallway to the basement where the telegraphers were waiting.

Meanwhile, back in the Oval Office, Grant lit another
cigar and leaned back in his chair. He looked at his attorney general with eyes narrowed against the wreathing
Havana smoke.

'Well, Charles,' he said. '*Les jeux sont fait.*'

'Yes, sir,' said the attorney general. He couldn't bring
himself to call Grant Ulysses, and he had never met
anyone who did. 'It's done.'

'You know what they say now, Charles.'

The attorney general nodded.

'*Rien ne va plus,*' he said quietly. 'No more bets.'

They didn't have long to wait.

John Barclay, U.S. marshal of the Wyoming Territory, sent the word through about eight hours later – just four hours short of the deadline. The telegraph line between Laramie and Cheyenne had suddenly become operative again – it didn't take a genius to figure out that it was the renegades who'd cut it – and the telegraph key in the railroad depot at Cheyenne had chattered out its staccato message. Barclay had then transmitted it direct to Washington, and it reached the president as he and his attorney general were drinking great mugs of the hot, strong coffee on which some people swore Grant lived. Others said it was whiskey, and the attorney general couldn't help but wonder whether Grant actually liked this awful brew: it tasted like thinned-down ship varnish and he said so.

'Coffee's no good unless the spoon'll stand up in it, Charles,' Grant grinned. 'You're getting effete.'

'I'm getting a bellyache,' his visitor said inelegantly. 'Haven't you got any whiskey?'

Before Grant could reply, there was a discreet knock and the young aide who had taken the president's message earlier came into the room. He had a sheet of paper in his hand which he passed wordlessly over the president's desk.

'The reply, sir,' he said. 'From Cheyenne.' He pronounced it Shy-enn, the way Easterners do.

'Good, good,' Grant said, getting up and taking the paper from him. 'That's all, Edward. Thank you.'

'Sir,' Edward said, going out. Grant didn't even look at him, so intent was he upon the contents of the transcription. Without comment he handed it to the attorney general.

THE MONEY IS TO BE SENT BY SPECIAL TRAIN TO CHEYENNE TO ARRIVE AT NOON ON OCTO-BER 5. AT NOON IN THAT DAY IT IS TO BE PLACED IN A ONE-HORSE BUGGY DRIVEN BY ONE MAN ALONE. HE WILL PROCEED TO HORSE CREEK CROSSING, TWENTY-SEVEN MILES NORTHWEST OF CHEYENNE, UNHAR-NESS THE HORSE, AND RIDE IT BACK TO CHEYENNE, LEAVING THE BUGGY WITH THE MONEY IN IT AT THE CROSSING. THE ENTIRE PROCEEDINGS WILL BE CAREFULLY OBSERVED BY US. ANY DEVIATION FROM THESE INSTRUC-TIONS WILL RESULT IN THE IMMEDIATE DESTRUCTION OF THE FREEDOM TRAIN. IF THEY ARE FOLLOWED EXPLICITLY THE FREE-DOM TRAIN WILL BE RELEASED AT MIDNIGHT ON OCTOBER 5. ANY ATTEMPT TO PURSUE HARASS OR CAPTURE MYSELF OR ANY OF MY PEOPLE DURING THE CONSUMMATION OF THESE ARRANGEMENTS WILL BE CONSIDERED A VIOLATION OF THE AGREEMENT AND THE TRAIN WILL BE DESTROYED.

The attorney general looked up to find President Grant watching him closely for a reaction.

'He's giving us no time to set anything up,' he said. 'Very smart. Very professional. Almost as if he knows what our reactions will be before we have them.'

'I don't want to hear how clever the sonofabitch is!' snapped Grant. 'I want to know how we're going to stop him from walking away with a quarter of a million dollars of taxpayer's money!'

During the waiting period, instructions had been passed to the Treasury Department to prepare the ransom money as Willowfield had instructed: a quarter of a million dollars, no single bill larger than fifty dollars. It made two quite substantial bundles. The attorney general had also sent a message across to his own office in the big old building on Pennsylvania Avenue. There was much to be done and he told the president so.

'We have to move fast now,' he said. 'A special train, I think. Engine tender and caboose, nothing more. Top priority clearance all along the line from the railroad people—'

'I'll see to that,' Grant nodded.

'Two of my men as guards for the money,' the attorney general continued. 'One of them to go out to, where was it? Horse Creek Crossing with the buggy, the other to lie low and pick up the trail of this Willowfield as soon as the Freedom Train has been released.'

'Good,' Grant nodded. 'You think we've a chance of stopping this man, Charles? Bringing him in?'

'We have a chance, sir,' the attorney general said. 'How good a chance I wouldn't care to say.'

'Then you'd best make damned sure you've got your best two men on that train, Charles.'

'I've already started the ball rolling,' the attorney general said.

'Your very best men, mind,' Grant insisted.

'Frank Angel,' the attorney general said. 'And Bob Little.'

'Little and who?' Grant said.

'Angel, sir. Frank Angel. One of my very best men.'

'That's a hell of a name for one of your people, Charles.'

'Yes, sir,' the attorney general said. 'I took the liberty of sending for Little, sir. He's waiting outside.'

'Good,' Grant said. 'Wheel him in.'

The attorney general got up and went to the door, holding it open for Bob Little, who had been waiting in the anteroom. He was a big, rangy man with corn-yellow hair and an open, farm boy's face. When he smiled he had the look of a mischievous schoolboy. He could not have looked less like a killer, but Grant knew that all of the Justice Department's special investigators were taught the killing arts, and if the attorney general said Little was a top man, it meant he was about as good a man as could be found anywhere in these United States. After the introductions, Little listened carefully as the details of his mission were outlined. Both the president and the attorney general confessed their misgivings about the whole business, their unease at sending him into such an open-ended situation.

'I can't tell you what to do or how to do it, Bob,' the attorney general said. 'Only that, no matter what, Willowfield's not to be allowed to walk away with that money. I'm going to suggest that you take Frank Angel along as your backup. You ride the buggy out to the rendezvous. Angel can pick up the trail, and then you can play the rest as you find it. Of course,' he said, gently, 'you can choose your own backup. It doesn't have to be Angel if you'd prefer someone else.'

Bob Little grinned his schoolboy grin. 'No, sir,' he said. 'Angel'd be fine. Can't think of anybody I'd rather have along.'

'Good,' said the attorney general. 'Take Angel. And get going.'

THREE

It could just about be done, the experts said.

They shook their heads over the time element, then allowed – albeit reluctantly – that whatever else Willowfield might be, he seemed to know with almost uncanny accuracy just exactly what the Union Pacific Railroad could do if it pulled out all the stops. And all the stops, by direct order of the President of the United States, were pulled all the way out. No expense, no effort was to be spared to get the two Justice Department men across the country in time to meet the deadline that Willowfield had set. UP's engineers figured it out on paper: a Special, using their fastest, most powerful locomotive with just a tender and one of the new lightweight cabooses, could rack up enough knots to cover the distance between Omaha and Cheyenne in the time that Willowfield had specified: as long as Little and Angel could be in Council Bluffs in time to make the connection.

So schedules were altered, switches thrown, trains diverted, stations closed, passengers discommoded, and a large number of Union Pacific personnel given unpleasant tasks at unholy hours in uncomfortable places. There were curses and complaints, there were threats and brandished fists, and later there were a couple of hundred very irate letters. But the train went through. The two Justice Department men got to Council Bluffs on time, and ten minutes after their arrival, the Special shunted out of the maze of yards, across the river, and away down the line on the start of its six hundred mile run toward the far mountains.

At Frank Angel's request, the Union Pacific had ferried Pat O'Connor eastward to meet their train, and the engineer, complaining every mile of the way at being taken away from his responsibilities, answered their questions as the Special bucketed down the line toward Cheyenne.

'Sure, it'd be hard to say how many men he had,' O'Connor said, replying to one of Bob Little's questions. 'I never seen more than four or five. How many he had up on the top of the Cut, I'd only be able to guess.'

'Did you hear any names used?' Angel asked him.

'Never a one,' O'Connor said. 'They weren't much on talking.'

He surveyed his inquisitors with wary suspicion. He'd heard that the Justice Department was sending out two of its men with the ransom for the Freedom Train – that much was already common railroad gossip. If you wanted the truth of it, it was also common railroad gossip that the Justice Department was off its head: what was needed for those barefaced thieves in Sweetwater Cut was a squadron of cavalry with a Gatlin gun. Sending two men, however capable-looking they might be, was another indication that politicians back east had no real conception of conditions out west, or just how tough a gang of cold-blooded killers like Willowfield's bunch could be.

This Angel, now, O'Connor thought. (Angel! That was a name for a fighting man, b'God!) Tall, he was, with eyes that would make a man think twice about making any jokes on the subject of angels. Broad in the shoulders and narrow at the hip, Angel had the contained, capable look of a trained athlete. He wore a dark blue shirt, corduroy pants tucked into the tops of mule-ear boots that, even if they were well kept, had seen better days. A cord coat in the same brown as the pants, a snug-fitting holster with a Frontier Colt. Face tanned, the cheekbones high enough to give Angel's face an angular look. Hair streaked, sun-bleached blond, cut fashionably long but not ostentatiously long like the self-styled frontiersmen O'Connor had seen strutting around the squares of midwestern cities, the type who got all their verisimilitude from dime novels. Angel looked like he might be some sort of engineer, a man who worked outdoors but not with his hands. The other one, Little, had the same kind of look. Except that where Angel spoke with a soft, clear drawl, Little's voice was slurred with the treacly vowels of the South. O'Connor, prideful of his ability to assess a man from his looks, tabbed Bob Little as one of those men who do well in all sorts of sport, who make the school or college athletic team, whose big, beefy handsomeness inspires hero-worship in all the other kids, and long sighs among the young ladies. The type was peculiarly American: they all had the same regular white teeth, the same ready boyish smile, the same ambling amiability. They usually ended up, O'Connor thought, with a small man's satisfaction, with the same hanging gut, the same false-hearty slap-on-the-back lifestyle, and the same sweet, small shrewish wife. Little didn't look like he was that far down the road yet, but he had all the outward appearances of the all-American boy.

O'Connor was about as wrong as a man could get.

Bob Little was, in fact, one of the three special investigators working for the Justice Department in whom the attorney general reposed complete trust. His amiable exterior concealed reflexes like a cobra's and he had a brilliant mind. He spoke four languages, was a champion swimmer, and like Frank Angel, he was used to being sent into trouble spots without back-up and often without even a briefing, his instructions brutally simple: *clean it up.*

There was a famous story about the Justice Department's investigators (later appropriated by the Texas Rangers) originating at a time when the attorney general had sent one of his men down to Lincoln county in New Mexico, where all the signs pointed to the outbreak of a civil war between the Anglos and the Spanish-American population. Later to be known as the Harrell War, it was, in 1873, just another of those headaches that frequently landed on the big desk in the echoing old building on Pennsylvania Avenue – the headquarters of the Department of Justice. On the documentation had been the presidential squiggle which meant: take care of this.

The attorney general had done what he always did: sent one of his special investigators down to the New Mexico Territory. He so reported to the president.

'What?' Grant had exploded. 'You did what?'

The attorney general repeated his statement that he'd sent one of his men down to look into the affair.

'You only sent one man?' Grant asked, aghast.

'Why, yes, sir,' the attorney general said, his eyebrows rising a centimeter higher. 'They only have one war, don't they?'

Justice Department investigators were a breed apart. Their existence was not advertised, nor did the attorney general supply the General Services Administration with a detailed breakdown in his departmental budget of what the expenses listed as 'Training of Special Staff' actually covered. They were picked men, trained to the peak of performance by a series of courses designed to create what the attorney general had envisaged: a thinking killing-machine.

No man who bore the title special investigator was allowed out into the field until he passed the battery of tests devised by the dour Armorer, himself one of the finest shots in the United States, a man who had forgotten more about weaponry than most others would ever learn. After him, trainees were passed along to the little Korean, Kee Lai, who taught unarmed combat and the martial arts of the Orient. He taught them how to kill with the edge of the hand, the way to find and paralyze the nervous centers of the human body, and how to survive the unexpected assassin. After that there were long hours with the man they called 'the Indian,' who was said to be good enough with a knife to take on armed men and come through alive. He taught them how to look after their weapons, how to heft them and throw them, how to place them hard into the human body so that no bone would deflect their thrust and they would kill the first time every time.

There was other training, too. Survival training, tracking, fieldwork. And more cerebral pursuits: a full and thorough basic grounding in law, the taking and presentation of testimony, the composition, duties and responsibilities of grand juries, military courts-martial and much-more. The attorney general had wanted thinking killing-machines. When the training was complete he had them.

Put a gun, a knife, a club in the hands of one of these men and they could use them, better than most. Given the additional quality of intelligence and training, they also knew a much more important thing: when not to. They were taught one basic rule: survive.

Of course, there was no way that Pat O'Connor could have known all this. To him, Frank Angel and Bob Little were a couple of well-built civil servants and if he let his impatience with these city boys show through once in awhile, it was only understandable. He explained, all over again, how the train had been held up. How Willowfield had sent him in to Cheyenne with the letter to be handed to the U.S. marshal. And how he'd been told to be sure and tell the marshal not to do anything hasty until the letter had been transmitted east.

'This Willowfield,' Little asked. 'How does he speak?'

'Jeez an' I must have told that twenty times already,' O'Connor said. 'Have you boys got any idea at all how many times I've been asked all this?'

'Tell us anyway,' Angel said.

'Jehosophat!' O'Connor said, exasperation plain in his voice.

'Son of Asa,' Little recited. 'King of Judah. Defeated by the Moabites, Ammonites, and Edomites about 900 B.C.'

Pat O'Connor looked at the big man as though he had just turned into a giraffe. Little grinned.

'Sure, it's a Bible scholar ycz are,' O'Connor said, his face setting. 'Now that'll go well on a job like this.'

'Patrick,' Angel said gently. 'Your prejudice is showing.'

'Aye, so it is,' O'Connor said. 'But all the same. . . .'

'The way of his speaking,' Little reminded him.

'I know it, I know it,' O'Connor flared. 'Sure an' I'll tell yez if ye'll give me but a moment.'

They gave him his moment and he used it to pull out a blackened clay pipe from the pocket of his navy-blue donkey jacket.

'English, it was,' he said, as he unrolled a yellow oilskin tobacco pouch and stuffed dark, oily looking shag into the bowl of the pipe.

'You mean British English, Pat?' Angel asked.

'Now, then,' O'Connor said, puffing furiously away at the pipe, which emitted great clouds of pungent smoke. 'Is there another kind?'

'An Englishman,' Little said, thoughtfully.

'Well, now and I never said that,' O'Connor said. 'I said the way of his speakin' 'twas English. As if he'd maybe come from there. But I'd not swear to even that.'

'Maybe English-born,' Angel said. 'But raised here.'

'Could be,' Little said. He asked O'Connor another question.

'Me tobacco?' O'Connor said, surprised. 'Sure, I buy it in Kansas City. By the pound. Why?'

'Oh, nothing,' Little grinned. 'We just wondered if someone we know gets his cigars from the same place.'

'Sure as hell smells like it,' Angel smiled back.

O'Connor stared at them, as if finally convinced that they were quite mad. He had no way of appreciating their private joke about the attorney general's famous cigars, and the Department story that he had them specially made from yak droppings laced with skunk-juice.

They heard the steady thunder of the driving wheels change rhythm slightly and the lurch as they went into a long bend. There was a deep rolling continuous boom of sound from beneath them. They looked at O'Connor.

'North Platte,' he said. 'We're making damned good time.'

The Justice Department men didn't need to comment. Both of them knew this part of the country well, and knew, just as if they were looking at a map, that the UP tracks

33

described a figure like an elongated S lying face down, Omaha to Grand Island to North Platte, where the rails crossed the wide northern fork of the Platte River – half a mile wide, and half an inch deep, as the old wagonmasters had used to say – over a long wooden trestle bridge. They also knew that they were already a good two-thirds of the way to their destination. Ahead lay Ogallala and Julesburg, one or two tank towns: nothing much before Cheyenne.

Pat O'Connor looked at the big railroad watch he'd taken from his vest pocket and nodded, yawning ostentatiously.

'What time is it?' Angel asked him.

'Five,' O'Connor said, and then again as if realizing what he had said and doubting his own good sense. '5 A.M.'

'Might get a couple of hours shut-eye,' Angel said.

'Aye,' O'Connor said. 'We'll be in Cheyenne by ten. I think I'll just get me head down awhile.'

They were the last words he ever spoke. He hunched himself down in the hard cot rigged along the wall of the caboose, and he was still there, trying to snatch a half-sleep, when Willowfield and his men blew the Special right off the tracks about forty miles on the far side of Julesburg.

FOUR

Willowfield's plan had been simple.

He didn't want the Freedom Train, nor anything in it. What could a man do with such dross – worthless souvenirs of a pointless history? No, the Freedom Train had served its purpose, and once he had secured presidential agreement that the ransom would be paid, he had abandoned it. He had recruited a band of drifters, helter-skelter rogues who knew nothing of the ransom or the other part of his plan. Once the hold-up had been effected, he had paid them off and they had dispersed. Around him Willowfield kept only the men he had picked as the core of his operation, the ones he had gathered together after he had decided to stop the Freedom Train.

They had left fires burning on the rim of Sweetwater Cut, dummies propped up on sticks guarding the beleaguered train. The boy-soldiers had been disarmed and suitably impressed with the necessity of doing nothing which would provoke the destruction of the Freedom Train. Then, laughing among themselves, Willowfield and his men had sifted out, moving down the long timbered slopes eastward toward Julesburg. It didn't matter anymore whether the soldiers discovered the ruse or not. There was nowhere they could go, no action they could take that would interfere with the completion of Willowfield's plan, and he led his men eastward without haste.

They were all good men, but not too good. He had his own reasons for wanting them to be just good enough. Willowfield was a fair judge of a man's reactions to given stimuli, and he'd picked them on that basis: his 'lieutenant,' Falco, Davy Livermoor, Hank Kuden, Gil Curtis, and even Buddy McLennon. Buddy was a rather more special choice, but the rule still applied: Willowfield never let sentiment interfere with business.

Chris Falco, the first of his recruits, he'd found guarding a tinhorn monte dealer in a Wichita deadfall, a tall, good-looking man with wings of gray hair alongside his head that made him look older, more distinguished than a paid gun had any right to look. Davy Livermoor had come up from Texas with a herd of long-horns which he'd sold to a buyer from the East for a good price. He'd joined up with Willowfield rather than go back and face the man whose herd it was and explain how he'd spent the money on Kansas City whores, lavish hotel suites, hand-cut suits, and hand-rolled cigars – a half year of riotous living that was coming to its inglorious end when Willowfield ran across him. Kuden, born Kudenheim in Stuttgart, Germany, was a former mercenary who'd emigrated to America a jump and a half ahead of the German police (who wanted to question him about a duel in which the young son of a noble *Graf* had died). His cropped head and scarred cheeks proclaimed his nationality, and six years in America had hardly softened the edge of his accent. He was a ruthless and unquestioning killer. Gil Curtis was one of Falco's finds. Falco had said Curtis was tops with explosives, and if Falco vouched for Curtis then that was all right with Willowfield. After all, Falco accepted his recommendations without question. Falco even tolerated Buddy McLennon, whom Willowfield had introduced as his traveling companion. Neither he nor any of the others talked with the boy, who in turn kept apart from them. He was just there, like one of the horses. As long as Willowfield paid the freight, they reckoned, they could turn a blind eye to his private life.

And Willowfield paid lavishly. He had learned a long time ago that in life everything had to be paid for. You paid in money, or blood, or sweat, or time; but you paid. The easiest way was money. With money you could get anything you needed out of life. When he needed information, he simply bought it. He had never encountered a man who could not be bought, one way or another. Some wanted dollars in their hands; others wanted what the dollars would buy: baubles, or women, or property. The loot, which he had salted away during his years of plundering during War, was more than enough to finance and support his contention, and to pay the small price needed to ensure the loyalty of such as Falco and the rest. He needed little himself, and that little was also easily bought.

A lifetime study of criminals had convinced Willowfield that their most besetting fault was a lack of imagination. They simply did not think big enough. You never made any sort of a killing if you tried to pinch pennies on the set-up. But if you were prepared to think on a really grand scale, there was no limit to what you could do. Thus it was that when he had first heard of the plans for the Freedom Train – a small item in a newspaper in San Francisco – he had realized, as if it had been preordained, that here was his opportunity, here the means of effecting, in one fell swoop, a coup that would provide him with the kind of money that few people even so much as see during an entire lifetime – enough money for the rest of his life. He went about his planning with a diligence and zeal that would have exhausted a man twenty years his junior. He plotted and planned, bribed and bought, hired and stole when and as he needed. He invested all of his time, all of his not-inconsiderable intelligence, all of his abilities to learning everything there was to about the Freedom Train: its routes, its history, its composition, its personnel. Then he set about learning the various ways in which, given the appropriate stimulus, the Union Pacific Railroad could, and would, respond to an emergency of the kind he had in mind.

Then, knowing what he knew, it became child's play to forecast with reasonable assurance the probable arrival time of the special train which would be used to send the ransom money to Cheyenne. It was easy to establish that the money would be in the charge of two men from the Department of Justice, that one of the engineers from the Freedom Train had been sped east to join them and – no doubt – to brief them upon the robbery and its perpetrators. All exactly as he had expected. Officialdom is by definition stupid, slow-moving, since its brain is a collective one. One man alone, ready to make rapid decisions and to act upon them immediately, must always be superior to officialdom, can always outwit it – since he can move faster, think faster and best of all, disappear faster. Even after he paid each of his men, he would still have enough to provide him with a good life for the remainder of his days. New Orleans, perhaps. Even Europe. He smiled his wounded smile and gave the order to destroy the Special.

They could hear her a long time before she came into sight, a long time before she ran up on to the embankment where Gil Curtis had planted the dynamite. Then she came thundering along the right of way, the bright glow from her smokestack projecting an orange glow onto the lowering dawn clouds. The raised embankment ran along the flank of a gully like a shelf, falling away below the train in a precipitous slope that was scarred with rock slides and shale. It ended, forty feet below, where the ground swelled upwards again toward the hills on the far side of the creek that sluiced down the valley. Curtis let the Special get all the way onto the embankment, the caboose rocking as she whammed past his marker. He slammed the plunger into the box. The flat smack of the explosion hit their ears an instant after they saw the brilliant blue-yellow light beneath the engine, and for a fraction of a second, the watchers thought the attempt had failed. Then they saw how the engine was leaning, nosing down, the front bogey completely destroyed, the bright brass reflector lamp crashing, smashing, digging, tearing into the ties with an enormous, deafening roar. Huge chunks of rock and earth and shattered timber flew high into the air over the shoulder of the thundering locomotive and then the whole terrifying juggernaut of metal and wood and flying rock erupted in an astonishing booming burst of fire that lofted great steel plates from the ruptured boiler up into the air like playing cards. The blast whirled across toward the hidden men, making the horses curvet in panic. They felt the long soft insistent pressure on their ears but they could not tear their eyes away from the terrible sight of the train ripping off the tracks and plunging down the side of the rocky gully. They heard the huge noise of the disintegrating engine sounding like the last quivering clangor of the great bell of Hades, the tender and caboose rolling over and over, breaking up as they rolled, and then the locomotive jumping up off the rocky slope and turning over, and over, and then, in a final, searing, stunning explosion of boiling flame, ending its life in the scoured, smoking pit it had dug for itself at the bottom of the gully.

'Jesus,' Falco said, into the comparative silence. His voice stirred Willowfield from the hypnotized reverie into which he had sunk. Then the fat man swung up into the saddle. The horse braced itself as his weight settled into the fork, and he pulled its head around to face downhill.

'Will she blow again?' he asked Curtis.

'Naw,' Curtis said, dancing triumph over what he had just effected still lighting the darkness of his eyes. 'That war the boiler went, Cunnel. She's done fer.'

'Good,' Willowfield said. 'Let's get down there.' He kicked the horse into a walk and led off across the broken ground toward the wreck. The bright yellow glow of the flames flickering over the hulk of the shattered engine reflected on the receding clouds. Hesitantly, somewhere in the smoking depths, a bird began to sing.

When Frank Angel opened his eyes he thought he was in Hell. The red glare of the flames, the charred stink of the burned ground, the crackling heat that brittled his skin all struck his senses simultaneously, muddling his mind. Fire? He could not remember anything. His mind was completely disoriented and his memory drowned in dread. Instinct told him to move. He could feel the scorch of fire, realized he was inside something that was burning. A broken wooden crate, his blurring eyes reported, seeing broken slatting, wood, twisted metal. He tried to move, and felt something pinning down his legs. He rolled back, kicking away the piece of timber that lay across them. As he did so, what was left of Bob Little's tattered body rolled away from him and slid down the canted floor.

It all came back to him then and he lay on the charring floor retching, oblivious. After a few minutes he was able to sit up, and the adrenalin surged through his veins: he knew he had to move. The train had been dynamited, and that meant whoever had dynamited it would be coming to inspect the results. If they found him alive they would kill him. He knew there was nothing he could do for Little, or for anyone else who had been on the train. The way the train had been destroyed was proof that the wreckers neither wanted nor expected survivors. He found his eyes were accustomed to the reddish glare, and looking around discovered that he was in a space between the collapsed wall and the upright-tilted floor of what had been the caboose. The wood was starting to smolder, and he could feel the heat of the flames on the other side of it. He went down on one knee, breathed deeply of the cooler air near the ground, and wormed through the A-shaped space. He came out into flickering red brightness, faced by the monstrous twisted jumble of the wrecked ten-wheeler. It lay on its back, one of the huge drive wheels still turning as it sought rest through gravitational pull. The entire body was torn apart like the throat of a lamb brought down by a pack of hunting wolves. Tongues of flame licked across the spilled oil and on the wood that had been trapped beneath the crushed tender. There was no sign of either the engineer or the fireman, and Angel knew that their chances of having survived both the explosion and the crash were virtually nonexistent. And O'Connor? If the little Irishman had come through the crash, he hoped O'Connor would have enough sense to keep his head down. The sound of horses moving on the shaley slope told him that any thought of going to look for the little

41

man was out of the question. Instead he moved on noiseless feet across the bed of the gully, away from the smoking wreck of the train. He splashed icy water on to his face, welcoming the sudden shock of it, then moved silently up a shelving slope toward a stand of pine thirty or forty feet away. The cool dampness of the ground was a welcome relief to his fire-dried skin, and he stretched his hands in the dew-damp grass. His shirt was full of small burned holes, his pants torn and filthy. His coat, with his wallet and money in it, had been hanging from a peg in the caboose, as had his gunbelt and sixgun. He cursed his own helplessness and eased back into the shadowed trees as he saw Willowfield lead his riders across the little creek and up to where the ruined train had ended its terrible downward plunge.

'Check around everywhere!' he heard one of the men shout. 'Make sure nobody's alive!'

'Find the safe first!' someone else shouted. Angel thought he detected the nasal twang of a British accent in the shouted command. Willowfield, he wondered? He wormed his way through the brambles and thicketed undergrowth until he reached a flattened bluff from which he could see down into the basin below without being seen.

The sun was coming up over the top of the mountains to the west now, sending long fingers of light that shafted through the trees like searchlights, paling the flickering flames that still licked stubbornly at the blackened wreckage, touching the wreathing smoke with pink fingers. Down below in the gully, Angel could see the men moving about. One of them sat on a horse: a gross, ugly man who waved his arms as he shouted commands to the others. Angel caught the timbre of the voice with its nasal twang, and knew that this must be Willowfield. Alongside the fat man was a tow-haired youngster on a fine piebald mare. He wore a pale blue shirt that shone in the sunlight, like silk. His close-fitting fawn pants were tight-tailored at crotch and rump. Angel noted the girlish shoulders, the androgynous hips and the full, pouting mouth almost clinically before turning his attention to a third man who was up on the sloping side of the gully shouting something.

'One off them alife up here!' he shouted.

Cropped bullet head, Angel noted, and the rigid upright stance of a soldier. He was standing over a hunched figure that lay on the slope where a break in the grass cover revealed the slate base beneath the thin mountain turf. As he watched, Angel saw the boy sitting next to Willowfield lay a hand on the fat man's forearm and say something. There was a plea in the way he looked at Willowfield, who nodded.

'Wait!' Willowfield shouted.

The man on the skyline nodded and shrugged, watching dispassionately as the boy kneed the piebald into a trot and headed across the foot of the gully until he was below where the bullet-headed one was standing. Then the boy got off the horse and went up the shale slide like a cat, eagerness in every line of his body. As he came up to the crest he slid a thin-bladed knife from a scabbard at his side, and Angel watched helplessly as the boy used it on the defenseless O'Connor. The Irishman's dying scream bounced off the rock walls of the gully as Angel bit back his own curse. The fat man had not moved; Angel thought he could see a smile on Willowfield's face as the boy ran down the slope and vaulted into the handsomely tooled saddle. He brought the piebald back alongside Willowfield and touched the fat man's pudgy hand, as if thanking him.

Willowfield nodded, a Roman emperor indulging his favorite.

'Colonel!'

The shout came from high up and off to the left of where the dead body of Pat O'Connor lay in the gullied shale. Angel could see a tall, broad-shouldered man who wore his holster low on the right and whose black hair was winged with gray from ear to crown. The man waved an arm.

'Colonel, I found the safe!'

'Get Gil over there, Chris!' Willowfield shouted back. 'Let him handle it!'

The man called Chris waved acknowledgment and yelled something. Another man came scrambling up the side of the gully, a canvas tote bag in his left hand.

Gil, Angel thought. He'd be the explosives man, the one who'd blown up the train. Medium height, slim, long black hair, and dark, deep-set eyes. The man wore greasy buckskin pants and a leather jacket. Gun on the left. No knife visible, but that didn't mean anything. Angel watched Gil go over the crest and out of sight with the one called Chris. As they did, two others came into sight and moved down the hill to where Willowfield sat, smiling slightly like some obscene Buddha, his horse shifting its feet as if to redistribute his weight. One of the men was short and thickset, running slightly toward overweight: thin black hair, slicked back, and a flat crowned Stetson hanging down his back on a leather loop around the neck. Highheeled boots – a cattleman, Angel thought – maybe a horsebreaker. The second man was the bullet-headed one with the German accent. He watched the man swing aboard a big bay tethered to a bush near where Willowfield sat. Scarred face, as if the man had been

44

involved in knife fights. An Army holster with the top flap cut away, the Army model Colt held in with a looped leather thong. No cartridges on the belt. A military man, Angel thought: he'd have his cartridges in a pouch from years of habit. The man's boots shone from polishing, and his saddle was in good shape, soaped and shined. Soldier, Angel dubbed him. He had given them all working names, to remember them by. Willowfield, Chris, the one with the gray hair. Gil the dynamiter. Texas, the one with the high-heeled boots. And the kid. There was a name for him, too, but Angel didn't use it.

The flat, damp sound of a small explosion echoed off the rocks behind the crest where Chris and Gil had disappeared, and a fat puff of black-gray smoke ballooned upward, thinning as it rose, disappearing in the morning breeze. Then the big man, Chris, came over the shaley crest swinging one of the gray canvas satchels, which contained, as Angel knew only too well, half of the $250,000 ransom. Behind Chris was Gil, lugging the second satchel. They scrambled down the slope and across the littered gully to where Willowfield sat waiting.

'Well done, boys,' the fat man said, a gloat in his voice. 'Well done.' He pulled one of the satchels open, his eyes flaring at the sight of the money inside.

'We goin' to share it out here, Colonel?' Chris asked.

'Oh, no,' Willowfield said. 'Not here.'

'We oughta get clear o' here pretty sharp, Colonel,' Texas said. 'No tellin' who mighta heard that train blow.'

'You underestimate me, my dear chap,' Willowfield said. 'I selected this place because there isn't so much as a sod-roofed dugout within ten miles of it. We shall move on, but not because we have to.' He turned to Chris. 'Did you, ah, check to make sure that nobody. . . ?'

He left it unsaid. Chris knew what he meant.

'We found four dead men and the one – the last one,' he said. 'I guess that was the crew. Engineer, fireman, brakeman, and two guards. Just like you said, Colonel.'

Willowfield nodded, as though mildly flattered at Chris's acknowledgment of the accuracy of his estimate. He took one last long, lingering look at the destruction he had caused, the havoc of twisted steel and broken rock, of trees torn out by their roots, and the great slicing gouged black scar down the side of the gully where the engine had plunged to its doom.

'Very well,' he said.

He kicked his horse into a walk, and the others fell into line astern.

In ten minutes they were out of sight, and the only thing moving in the gully was Frank Angel. He picked his way carefully through the wreckage, trying to find the things he would need to stay alive. He did not allow himself the luxury of anger at the death of Little, or bitterness because he had been unable to prevent the callous, casual murder of Patrick O'Connor. His first task was to survive.

It took him three hours to find what he needed: some money, a sixgun, a canteen full of sweet water. By high noon he was following the tracks of Willowfield's party. He had names for all of them now, and that was enough. He was a long way behind them, and afoot, but he had one advantage: they didn't know he was on their back trail.

FIVE

He walked almost a full day.

The tracks he was dogging led off in a long curve that first had him thinking they must be heading for Cheyenne, but then he realized that they were keeping to roughly the same trace as the old Fort Morgan road that would eventually lead them up into the mountains of Colorado and to the city of Denver.

It was hard going on foot. The land which looked so flat and drab from the windows of a speeding train was anything but flat, anything but featureless. It was crissed and crossed by washes and gullies, narrow hogbacks and long rising slopes, folding up and down like the surface of the sea. Even this late in the year the sun was hot and unfriendly, and it made the walking hard work. Head down, not thinking about distances or speed, Angel stumbled on, antlike in the empty wilderness, hour after endless hour until he came to the crest of a long descending slope, and at the foot of it saw Kitchen's ranch.

Henny Kitchen was a pernickety old loner with the permanently bowed legs and muscular arms of a man who has spent his life on horseback; his skin was the color and texture of saddle leather and his scraggy beard was a salt-and-pepper mixture of colors: gray and brown and white.

He watched Angel come down the long slope, his shrewd pale eyes narrowed, keeping the stumbling figure covered with the cocked Henry rifle he had gone ostentatiously into the cabin to fetch. When Angel got near enough for him to see the walking man's condition, Kitchen laid down the rifle with an exasperated grunt and hurried to help the approaching man.

Within an hour, Angel was sitting in a big old horsehair-stuffed chair with his feet propped up. Kitchen had bathed him, slapped some strong-smelling salve on his burns, spooned a steaming bowlful of what tasted like deer stew into his unprotesting mouth, and topped that up with two mugs of treacle-thick coffee and as many slugs of snakehead whiskey.

'B'Gawd an' Moses,' Kitchen said finally, sitting back on his haunches and squinting at his patient. 'Do b'lieve you'll live, boyo.' Angel managed a grin.

'Anyone who can survive two slugs of whatever was in that bottle isn't all that easy to kill off,' he said. 'What the hell was it?'

'He-he,' Kitchen snickered. 'Make 'er m'self. Pooty good stuff, hey?' He took a solid slug of the liquor himself, as if Angel had reminded him of its existence.

'Pooty good,' Angel grinned. He tried to sit up, and long slow pains pulsed through his body. 'Aaah,' he said, softly.

'You may be in a hurry, boyo,' Kitchen said. 'But you ain't goin' anyplace. What the hell was it hit you anyways, a train?'

Angel shook his head, startled for a moment by the accuracy of the old loner's guess. 'I got to move on, Mr Kitchen,' he said.

'Henny,' Kitchen said. 'Call me Henny. Listen, boyo,

48

you got more bruises on you than a feller been stampeded on. May even have a couple bones bruk for all I know. I ain't no medic. But I can tell you one thing – you ain't about to move on. No sir Matilda!'

'Listen,' Angel began, weakly. Kitchen ignored him.

'Y'ever hear about that feller in the Bible?' Kitchen was saying, as he busied himself scouring out a pan with a stiff brush. 'Met Death on his way someplace. "Howdy," sez Death, polite as you please. "Jumpin' Jesus!" sez this feller, an' he takes off down the road like someone set fire to his ass. Death watches him go a-runnin', and shakes his head, sad-like. "What in tarnation's a-bitin' him, anyways?" Death sez. "He ain't got no reason to be afeared o' me today. It's tomorrow I got his appointment down for".'

He slapped his thigh, and looked up to see if Angel was listening. 'What d'ye think o'that, then?' he cackled.

There was no reply. Angel had already fallen asleep, and Kitchen let him sleep on until he woke naturally, around dawn, as the old man started clattering about to boil up some coffee and get the day up and moving.

'Well, well, Sleepin' Beauty awakes,' Kitchen grinned. 'How you feelin'?'

Angel sat up. He felt a damned sight better and he said so. He got up off the chair in which he'd slept, easing his stiffened legs. He grimaced as his feet touched the floor, and remembered how swollen they had been. He wasn't accustomed to that kind of walking. After he'd hobbled about for a few minutes, he began to feel halfway normal and asked Kitchen some questions as he nursed the tin mug of coffee that the old man handed him.

'Five o' them, you say?' Kitchen mused.

Angel nodded, and repeated the description of the fat man.

'One o' them had gray hair alongside his head, so,' he told Kitchen, using his hands to describe Falco's distinctive hair. 'Another one was short, tubby-lookin'. Might've been a Texan.'

'Naw, boyo,' Kitchen said. 'I'd sure as hell recall seein' a bunch like that. Mind you, if they was headin' for Denver like you say, they'd probably cut over in back o' the hills toward Fort Morgan, bed down there a night.'

'They might have swung north,' Angel hazarded a guess.

'Not damn' likely,' Kitchen contradicted. 'Nothin' up there but ten thousand hostiles with blood in their eye. They'd be double-damn fools if they wuz to head north.'

Angel nodded. Since the Custer disaster in June, Wyoming, Montana, and even Idaho were dangerous territories to traverse. Sioux, Cheyenne, Arapaho, all the Plains tribes were in an incendiary mood and a small band of men, no matter how well-armed, would not get far across their lands. They had been promised their hunting grounds for as long as the grass grew, and it looked as if they were planning to keep them – any damned way they could.

More than that, though: there was nowhere up there for Willowfield and his gang to go. Men with money burning holes in their jeans would head for a big town where they could find bright lights, soft beds, willing women. The nearest supply of those would be in Denver and it was on Denver he decided to bet his roll.

Kitchen made a living trading horses. He bought badly used animals from trailherders at Ogallala or the Army at Fort Sedgwick, paying a few dollars a head. Then he would drive the animals to his place and nurse them back to health. Most of the time he was able to do such a good job that he could sell them back to the Army at a handsome profit. It gave his contrary soul pleasure to take money from the same people who had abandoned the horses as useless. He was happy to sell Angel a big rangy roan with powerful shoulders and legs that looked sturdy enough to do farm work. They worked out a deal that included an old McLellan saddle, a bedroll, and a bridle, but Kitchen wouldn't take a cent for his hospitality.

'Hell's teeth, boyo,' he said. 'Pleasure to have somebody to yatter at. You sure you're in shape to ride?'

'No, I'm not,' Angel said, managing a grin. 'But I aim to get at it anyway.'

'You must want to ketch up with them jaspers real bad,' Kitchen observed. 'I wish you luck of it.'

'Thanks, Henny,' Angel said, meaning it. 'For everything.'

'Aw, go on an' git!' Kitchen said. He slapped the roan across the rump and the animal moved off at a trot, snorting with surprise. Kitchen stood watching as Angel lifted the horse's stride to a canter, and not until all he could see was the soft plume of dust marking the rider's passage did he turn away and return to his chores.

'B'Gawd an' Moses,' he muttered. 'Whoever them fellers is, I sure am glad I ain't one of 'em!'

He picked up their trail at Two Mile Creek.

A man who ran a small spread up on the divide, Dan Callow, remembered the fat man and the boy. He had sold the riders some grain for their horses, which they had paid for in good clean American greenbacks. Angel grinned at the thought of that as he headed the big roan up into the foothills. The trail ran along the south Platte, which looked about as muddy as usual – too thick to drink, too

51

thin to plow – and he could see it snaking up into the mountains ahead like a skein of string left unrolled behind some meandering wagon. The mountains lay ahead in rolling pile after soaring pinnacle, slate gray and deep purple, not the shining mountains of the summer but sullen, heavy, their peaks already capped with snow. He checked off in his mind the mountain torrents that raced down to the river whose trace he was now following: Cache-le-Poudre, Clear Creek, St. Vrain's Fork, Big Thompson, and Little Thompson. A man could take trout up there with his bare hands. The air was sharp, the sky clear. It felt good to be out in the open again: lately he had been too much in cities, and had missed the winey taste of the mountain air.

He camped overnight in a clearing that stood sheltered beneath a frowning stone bluff in the edge of the pine forest. Two wood pigeons – which advertised their presence by noisily calling each other in the woods – provided him with supper. He dug heavy clay from the river bank, making two heavy balls in which the whole bird, feathers and all, disappeared. These clay balls he laid in the glowing red center of his small fire, and waited until the clay was hard and brittle. Using a stick he rolled the clay balls out of the fire and let them cool slightly before tapping them, hard, with the barrel of his sixgun. The clay balls broke open, and the steaming pigeons, feathers stripped away by the baking, were ready to eat. He cleaned them swiftly with his knife and devoured the soft flesh with relish. He wished he had some beer. A glass of beer would have completed a meal that Delmonico's couldn't have improved. Next morning he pushed the roan harder, and made Denver halfway through the day. He walked the horse through the unlovely outskirts of the city, past the freighting corrals and teamster outfits, the tent shantie and the stockyards, the sawmills and the builder's merchants, making for the most famous rendezvous in Denver. This was a huge corral next to which stood a saloon called The Mammoth. It wasn't as big as its name claimed, and the immense, and not particularly accurate, painting of the creature from which the saloon took its name was peeled and faded on the unlovely false front. Nevertheless, the place was crowded at every hour of the day and night with incoming or departing travelers, wagon-masters looking for help, riders looking for work, people wanting to leave messages or pick them up, people hoping to buy or sell cattle or horses or mules or oxen or wagons or whatever goods they had carried this far and wished to carry no further. The place smelled like a stable. Angel bought himself a beer and moved around, listening, getting used to the noise and the sharp stink of sweat and tobacco again. Once or twice he stopped and asked someone a question, but usually met only a shrug, sometimes a shake of the head, once in a while a spoken negative. Nobody had seen his men. He drank another beer, and asked the bartender where the express office was. On Central, the man said, his face slick with perspiration; right next to the American Hotel.

He got on the roan and moved up Latimer Street toward Central. Denver had grown enormously, he thought, since it had sprung up from hastily sawed planks ripped from the flanks of Long's Peak about a decade ago. He wondered if the men who had made the first strikes up above Idaho Springs would recognize this part of the country if they saw it now. There were shops and stores and bazaars everywhere the eye moved: hardware, sporting goods, groceries, mining equipment, and dry goods jammed every which way in the gloomy interiors and spilling out on to the porched sidewalks beneath a jumbled rabble of signs and advertising come-ons, which defeated the eye they were supposed to attract. He saw one or two places that were selling Indian trinkets, Navajo silver, Ute jewelery. All along the boarded walks the scurrying, head-down mass of humanity ebbed and flowed like some strangely colored tide.

Trappers and hunters, long Hawken rifles or bundles of pelts slung on their shoulders, mingled with the crowd, their buckskins greasy and blackened from long seasons of thoughtless wear; bumping their shoulders were whey-faced asthmatics and consumptives come to breathe easier in the mile-high atmosphere of the city or to take what was known as the 'camp cure' – living as tough and rough as they could stand it up in the mountains, with guide and tent and wagon and stove until the fall closed in, then wintering in some hotel or boarding house until spring touched the flanks of the mountains once again with tender green fingers. Soldiers on leave swung by, spurs ajingle, swirling their long navy-blue serge capes dramatically. Teamsters moved their wagons up and down the muddy streets with strings of oaths like foreign tongues, oaths that would have reddened the ears of any decent woman had she heard them. Angel saw very few white women, very few women at all if you didn't count the Ute squaws bundled in blankets sitting impassively at the feet of their stone-faced spouses or trailing along the regulation three paces behind them. Up toward the center of town he saw dapperly dressed Fancy Dans, 'way-up' gamblers or confidence men, or both, jostled by burly, bearded ranchers made to look even huger by the massive buffalo-robe coats and leggins they affected.

The express office, with its Wells Fargo sign outside, was packed and he decided to take a rain check on sending his telegraph message. Another hour wasn't going to make that much difference, he thought: the news would be just as bad after lunch as it was now. He saw the sign of the American Hotel and decided to get something to eat. He was just crossing the lobby toward the dining room when he saw George Willowfield coming down the wide staircase.

SIX

It was just too damned good to be true.

Yet there the fat man was, elegantly dressed in a dark blue suit with a faint pinstripe, a gleaming white shirt, a cravat that looked like pure silk, and a stickpin that looked like a diamond, coming down the wide curving staircase of the American Hotel like he owned it. Angel turned away from the entrance to the dining room and made his way across the lobby toward the reception desk. There was no danger of Willowfield recognizing him: he'd never seen Angel, didn't even know he existed. Angel leaned against one of the marbled pillars by the desk and watched the fat man. He scanned the lobby for any sign of Willowfield's henchmen, but saw no familiar face. Willowfield made his way across the lobby and subsided into a well-upholstered wing chair set close to the fireplace. He rested his hands on top of his silver-capped cane, and rested his chin on his hands, gazing sightlessly into the fire.

Angel went across to the desk.

'Excuse me,' he said to the clerk. 'Isn't that Colonel Willowfield over there by the fire?'

The clerk followed Angel's gaze and smiled.

'That's correct, sir,' he said. 'Do you know the colonel?'

'Slightly,' Angel said. 'Are his friends still staying with him?'

'Ah, I, ah, beg your pardon, sir?' The clerk palmed the five dollars and his face was once more wreathed in smiles. 'His friends, ah, no, sir. They left yesterday, I believe. Would you like me to—?'

'Not now,' Angel said. He was already moving, walking purposefully across the lobby toward where Willowfield was sitting. The fat man's eyes flickered up to check him over, and then slid away. For a moment Angel could have sworn that there was satisfaction in them, but it wasn't possible. He took a seat opposite the fat man.

'Colonel,' he said.

George Willowfield raised his head slightly. He let his eyes rest on Angel, openly cataloging his travel-stained clothing, scuffed boots, unshaven jaw. He allowed Angel to see the contempt touch his expression and then looked away without speaking.

'If I was a gambling man,' Angel said, unperturbed, 'I'd say you just came into a lot of money, Colonel. Would I be right?'

Willowfield's head came up, sharply this time. His eyes were narrowed and he looked at Frank Angel warily, tension in his stance.

'What?' he said. 'What? Who are you, sir?'

Angel told him his name and where he was from. Willowfield looked at him for a long, silent moment, and then shook his head sadly.

'Too late, sir,' he said. 'You are too late.'

'Too late for what?'

'Mr Angel, you see before you a betrayed man,' Willowfield said.

'Oh, come on!' Angel snapped. 'Not that!'

'Alas, it's true,' Willowfield said. 'They took it all, Mr Angel. Every penny of it.'

'It had better be good, Willowfield,' Angel told him. 'Very, very good.'

'The truth, sir,' the fat man said heavily, 'is unassailable.'

'Try me,' Angel said, leaning back in the chair. 'Who was it – the boy?'

The fat man's face went a pasty white, and for a moment Willowfield's shock showed clearly on his face.

'What ... what do you know about the boy?' he croaked.

'I know about the boy,' Angel said. 'And Chris and the German. I know it all, Willowfield.'

'You ... you were on the train?' the fat man whispered. Then, with growing conviction, 'You were on the train.'

Angel nodded. The man's reactions were hardly what he had been expecting; Willowfield sounded almost relieved to hear what he had just told him.

'That's how you got here so fast,' Willowfield said. He said it like a man who has just had a conjuring trick explained to him.

'You want to tell me about it?' Angel prompted, harshly.

'Yes, of course,' Willowfield said. 'Of course. I planned it all so well. So perfectly. It was a perfect plan.'

'It was pretty good,' Angel agreed.

'Everything went like clockwork.'

'Until you got to Denver. Then your boys decided to change the scenario.'

'Change the scenario,' Willowfield nodded. 'Yes. They shamed me.'

'Go on.'

'We came up here two nights ago. We got in at night.'

'You all came here, to the American?'

'Yes. We were going to share out the money, then have a farewell dinner at the Alhambra or the Palace. Then. . . .'

'You started to share out the money?'

Willowfield nodded, as though unable to continue for a moment.

'Where was this?' Angel asked.

'Upstairs. In my suite. I'd promised them ten thousand each.'

'But when they saw you had a quarter of a million they decided to doublecross you.'

'Falco,' Willowfield said. 'It was Falco.'

Angel said nothing. He wasn't about to let Willowfield know how little he really knew about them.

'We were talking, laughing,' Willowfield said. 'I had the money ready. Ten thousand for each of them. Then Buddy. Buddy . . . he . . . oh, my God.'

His head fell and the mountainous shoulders heaved with remembered grief. Angel watched impassively as Willowfield got control of himself, blowing his nose on a huge white linen handkerchief. Several men in the lobby looked across at them curiously, but their gaze slid away when Angel stared at them.

'He had a knife,' Willowfield whispered. 'Buddy had a knife. He likes to use a knife.'

'Like he did when he killed the man after the wreck?' Angel guessed.

'Yes,' Willowfield said, confirming Angel's guess that Buddy was the name of the kid. 'He shamed me. In front of all of them. He made me beg for my life. He stripped me, mocked me, jeered at me. Then he made me beg. Beg!'

His voice trailed to a maudlin stop and his shoulders began to heave again. Then without warning the sniveling stopped and the big head came up. Willowfield's eyes were blazing with a malevolence so intense that Angel could almost smell the sulphur.

'They shamed me!' the fat man hissed. 'They robbed me, and reduced me to a groveling animal. They will pay for that. I will see each of them dead!'

'You may read about it someplace,' Angel said. 'But that's all.'

'No!' Willowfield snarled. 'I want them all dead. Especially the boy. Especially the boy!'

'Ask the judge,' Angel said.

Willowfield looked at him, and there was cunning and wariness mixed with the light of hatred behind his eyes, and something else, something Angel could not quite identify. Satisfaction? What had the fat man to gloat over? Angel watched as Willowfield drew in a long, slow breath and then leaned back in his chair, admiring the way the fat man got control of himself.

'Well, now,' Willowfield said. 'Let us examine the matter.'

'Let us,' Angel said. 'By all means.'

'You, Mr Angel, represent the Department of Justice, you said?'

'That's right '

'It is, I imagine, your allotted task to retrieve the stolen money and to bring the malefactors to the bar of justice.'

'Something like that '

'You were very quick,' Willowfield said. 'Much quicker than I expected. If you had been a few days longer, I would not have been here. I would have been on the trail of those . . . those *scum*, myself.'

'Instead of which,' Angel pointed out, 'You have other commitments.'

Willowfield steepled his fingers and touched them to his thin lips, and allowed a small smile to touch his face. He nodded, as though coming to a decision.

'So be it,' he said. 'You prevent me from pursuing Falco and the others. I would have remained behind them until either they or I were dead. Now I think I will let you do it for me.'

'How's that?' Angel said.

'My dear sir,' Willowfield said. 'If I tell you where they are heading, you will pursue them, will you not?'

'I will,' Angel said. 'And you know it.'

Willowfield nodded, standing up and putting his weight on the silver-topped cane. 'And myself, sir?'

'I'll hand you over to the United States marshal,' Angel told him. 'He can keep you on ice until you're shipped back east for trial.'

'Ah,' said Willowfield. 'You're efficient, Mr Angel. I can see that. A man after my own heart.'

'Yeah,' said Angel, getting up from his chair. 'Shall we walk across to the marshal's office, Colonel?'

'Oh, not yet, Mr Angel,' Willowfield said. 'Allow me to buy you lunch, sir. If you are to be the instrument of my revenge, I want to help you in every way I can. I will tell you all, Mr Angel, but pray let us talk in a civilized manner. Afterward, when we've eaten, we can walk across the street to the marshal and conclude this dreary matter. What do you say, sir?'

Angel looked at the fat man, and Willowfield met his gaze with an expectant, open smile.

'No tricks?' Angel said.

'My dear sir,' Willowfield smiled. 'Of course not. Come,

let us go into the dining room. They do a very fine steak here. Unless you prefer trout, of course. The *truite au bleu* is memorable, sir, quite memorable.'

You had to hand it to the old renegade, Angel thought: he had style.

SEVEN

Willowfield sang like a bird.

Angel identified himself to the United States marshal for Colorado, a tall, rangy man with the deep chest and sturdy legs of the mountain-born, and delivered the fat man into his custody. The marshal, whose name was John Henderson, was only too happy to assist the Justice Department by promising to keep Willowfield on ice until an escort could be sent out to take him back to Kansas City. Then Henderson commandeered the telegraph office, and stood by as Angel made his long initial report over the wires, ending it with the information that he had taken Willowfield and asking for an escort to take him east. It would be a while before a reply came through, and he spent the time talking to Willowfield, filling out the picture that the fat man had given him of the whole robbery and the men who had taken part in it.

Willowfield was more than willing to talk. He explained how he had dreamed up the idea of ransoming the Freedom Train, how he had worked out the ideal locale to stop the train, how he had recruited the men to effect his dream. He'd found Chris Falco bodyguarding a tinhorn whose dealing was no better than it had to be. A killer, Falco was, but he'd gotten away with a self-defense plea on the two occasions when the law had been involved. Gil Curtis, whom Falco had found, was a wizard with any kind of explosive. He'd learned his trade with the UP as it blasted its way through the Rockies, but decided to put his knowledge to more practical use. Curtis had blown safes in seven different parts of the States, and nobody had ever so much as lost a finger. Hank Kuden, whose real name was Hans Kudenheim, Willowfield had met back East: a dissatisfied soldier with a genius for timetabling and planning. Kuden could reduce any operation to a series of simple instructions that even a rabble of Mongolian peasants could understand and execute. Davy Livermoor had been recruited for two reasons: first, he was a fine tracker, but second, and more important, he still had 'respectable' bank accounts in Kansas City, and in Sedalia, Missouri. So not only was Davy their expert guide to every good and bad trail in the endless expanse between the Missouri and the Rio Grande, he was also a means through which the ransom money, if it was marked or recorded by serial number, could be 'laundered.' All they would have to do to check it out was to deposit some of the money in one of Davy's accounts, wait long enough for it to set off alarms, then send a mug in to withdraw some money. If he was taken, they would know the money was 'hot.' If not, they were home free.

Angel had asked where McLennon fit in.

'Ah, sir,' Willowfield had said, as if with huge regret. 'You choose to wound me with reminders of my own folly. I cherished that boy. Looked after him as if he were my own son. Gave him everything: the clothes on his back, the horse he rode, money to spend. You see how I am repaid for my generosity.'

He made a gesture that encompassed all the treachery

of mankind, and once again, Angel felt the small warning of disbelief touch his mind. It was all just too damned cut and dried, but he couldn't find a flaw in it. He had checked everything.

The messages started to come through from Washington, and not one of them had good news in it.

ANGEL. CARE U.S. MARSHAL, DENVER, COLO. SPECIAL CREW DISPATCHED SCENE WRECK. STOP. SEARCH OF FREEDOM TRAIN REVEALS APPARENT THEFT DECLARATION OF INDEPEN-DENCE STOP IMPERATIVE QUESTION WILLOW-FIELD REGARDING THIS. SQUEEZE HIM UNTIL HE SQUAWKS BUT GET ANSWERS URGENT STOP. NEED NOT TELL YOU DOCUMENT PRICE-LESS AND MUST UNDER NO CIRCUMSTANCE BE PUT AT RISK REPEAT NO CIRCUMSTANCE STOP TELEGRAPH REPORT EARLIEST STOP ATTORNEY GENERAL

Back, two hours later, went the reply.

ATTORNEY GENERAL. DEPARTMENT OF JUSTICE. WASHINGTON D.C.
WILLOWFIELD DENIES ANY KNOWLEDGE THEFT OF DOCUMENT OR ANYTHING ELSE FROM FREEDOM TRAIN STOP SAYS HIS ORDERS EXPLICITLY FORBADE ANY THEFT HISTORICAL ARTIFACTS WHICH WERE QUOTE WORTHLESS UNQUOTE STOP HE SUGGESTS AND I CONCUR THAT FALCO MIGHT HAVE DECIDED TAKE SOMETHING AS QUOTE ACE IN THE HOLE UNQUOTE STOP HAVE YOU ANYTHING IN OUR

RECORDS ON FIVE MEN NAMED MY FIRST
REPORT STOP
ANGEL

He waited in the express office for perhaps an hour, drinking coffee he didn't want, before the key began to chatter again, stuttering out its coded message as if venting some kind of mechanical spite. The telegrapher scrawled the words down as fast as they came through and handed the transcript to Angel. It looked like gobbledygook to the telegrapher, but Angel could read it almost without effort. The Department of Justice used a very simple one-letter-up code for telegraph transmissions. In it 'a' became 'b' and 'b' became 'c'; thus, the word 'cat' for instance was rendered 'dbu.' It prevented casual eyes from being privy to Department secrets. Angel read the message quickly.

ANGEL. CARE U.S. MARSHAL, DENVER, COLO. NO RECORD YOUR MEN HERE STOP ON BASIS YOUR REPORT MAKE URGENT PRIORITY PURSUIT AND CAPTURE NOT KILLING REPEAT NOT KILLING OF ANY OR ALL OF MEN INVOLVED IN ROBBERY STOP AGAIN REPEAT DO NOT UNDER ANY CIRCUMSTANCES PUT DOCUMENT AT RISK STOP ESCORT ARRANGED ARRIVING DENVER OCTOBER THIRTEENTH STOP NOTHING TO PREVENT YOUR IMMEDIATE COMMENCEMENT PURSUIT STOP STRESS ONCE MORE PARAMOUNT IMPORTANCE RECOVERY DOCUMENT UNHARMED STOP GOOD LUCK STOP
ATTORNEY GENERAL

'Well, thanks,' Angel said. 'Thanks a lot.'

It was really pretty country but he had no eyes for it. He pushed the horse hard, wanting only to get the last stage of the journey out of the way. He'd ridden a special train that Henderson had organized with the local manager of the D & RG, and run through the inky mountain night to Colorado Springs, where the engineer had slapped him on the back and wished him well as he led the roan down the slanting walkway out of the freight car and climbed into the saddle.

'Did they give you any hint of which way they were planning to go?' he'd asked Willowfield. The fat man had looked him straight in the eye and said no.

'I wish to God I knew,' he'd said fervently. 'I really do.'

'That's bad,' Angel said. 'They could be heading anywhere.' He got up to leave. There wasn't anything left to talk to Willowfield about. He'd have to take the chance that they'd headed south, and hope he could pick up a trace of them along the road. It was a thin chance at best.

'Wait,' the fat man said.

Angel stopped in the open doorway of the cell. The deputy, whose name was Jackman, stood with the keys in his hand, waiting to lock the door.

'I remember,' Willowfield said. His face puckered with the effort to recall the exact words he had heard.

'Falco,' he said. 'Mentioned getting fresh horses. At Canon City. Is there somewhere called Canon City?'

There was – and Angel was heading for it now. He figured he might have cut some time off their lead by commandeering the special train to the Springs. If they were planning to change horses in Canon City, they must be heading west for Durango, crossing the Sangre do

Cristos mountains at Poncha Pass and dropping down the long valley to Alamosa, where they could track the Rio Grande up into the San Juans, climb up to and over Wolf Creek Pass, and head on to Durango. It was a long, tough ride and they wouldn't be moving fast. Not for the first time, he wondered why they were making it.

So now he moved southward along the flanks of the mountains, his eyes assailed from every direction by riotous autumnal colors. The bright, bold green of cottonwood tress, the paler gold of the aspens, the sharp lemon yellow of wild grape vines heightened by the crimson spray of Virginia creeper and the dark glossy green of laurel, all set against the shattered face of the grim granite shoulders going up and up toward the invisible summit of Pike's Peak. Up there, fantastic jumbles of gargantuan boulders were lined and splashed with every conceivable hue: carmine, vermilion, brown, red, blue, gray, yellow, green ochre, a spectrum which would have defied duplication from the brush of a great artist – a dazzling chiaroscuro that awed the senses. As he bore toward the southwest, the scenery changed slowly. He was still climbing, imperceptibly, but gradually getting higher up to where the scenery became grimmer. Now the heavy dark blue shadows of pines lay upon the pale mountain grass, and the horse moved silently over a centuries-deep carpet of pine needles. The mountains soared in bare and lonely beauty away and away and beyond away, a vista of such grandeur that it made the breath catch in awe, reduced the puny mind and soul of man to insignificance. By nightfall, Angel was on a curving crest that curled away toward the west, with a long open plain sloping downward from it toward a meandering creek. On the far side of the creek was an unlovely huddle of buildings scattered along a

single street. One or two lights were already making
squares of yellow against the darkness. Far off in the blue
twilight the huge black bulk of Pike's Peak lay like a
sentient shadow against the night. Somewhere he could
hear a coyote yelping. It was already very cool.

'Canon City,' he told the horse. 'Garden spot of
Colorado.'

He gigged the roan into a trot, and the animal pricked
up his ears, anticipating the warm stable, food, and water.
Splashing through the shallow creek, Angel came up the
slope from the ford to where the straggling street began,
heading toward the biggest building he could see. He just
had time to make out the words Eldorado Saloon on the
lighted signboard above the porch before a blasting hail of
bullets smashed from the black maw of the alley on his
right.

EIGHT

He went over the side and hit the dirt.

Through the thunder of the shots he heard a high shrieking screech that went on and on as he rolled over and over through the roiling dust toward the partial shelter of a water trough outside one of the buildings on the left hand side of the street. The roan was on its back in the dust, arching its spine upward, legs flailing as it died in agony. Angel was already coming up on one knee with a gun in his hand. There was a numbness in his left hip that he had no time to try to identify, for now three men were coming out of the alley running, silhouetted briefly against the yellow lights, their guns snapping at him.

He heard a hoarse shout from somewhere up the street, the startled scream of a woman as he emptied his sixgun at the darker knot of movement where he calculated the running men would be, and he heard a sharp shout of sudden pain.

Desperately he thumbed shells through the loading gate of the Colt, eyes wary as a cornered cat, listening to the fading thump of running feet. There were no more shots and for a long minute the silence was immense. He could hear the kicked-up dust sifting sibilantly back to earth. The roan was already dead, a bulky blackness in the dark street. He thought he could see a small dark huddled shape beyond the horse, but he did not move, staying hunched down, the sixgun tilted and cocked ready, watching and watching.

There was commotion up the street and now he could see a group of men coming forward into the street from the well-lit porch of the saloon. One of them was a tall, heavily built man wearing a dark business suit with the pants tucked into high English-style riding boots. As the man strode down the street, light from a window glinted on the star pinned to the lapel of his coat. He holstered his sixgun and rose slowly from behind the water trough and, as he did, the man with the star whirled to face him, his hand coming up full of gun. Angel froze solid.

'Hold it right there, sonny,' the marshal snapped. There was a frayed edge of tension in his voice, and Angel tried very hard not to move a muscle. This middle-aged man with the drooping walrus mustache was strung up tighter than a banjo. If someone coughed he might pull the trigger of that enormous looking Navy Colt.

'Andy, you git that feller's gun!' the marshal said. One of the men behind him sidled toward Angel. The others fanned out in a half circle.

'Take it easy there, marshal,' Angel called. 'I'm the one got bushwhacked!'

'As to that,' the lawman retorted, 'we'll see. Andy, you hustle him over to my office. Two of you men bring that other feller. Easy with him, now. He ain't dead yet by the look of him. Somebody send for the Doc.'

The one called Andy was a short, weedy man with wispy blond hair and a weak mouth with cupid-bow lips that he licked nervously as he came up behind Angel. He wore ordinary blue denim pants and a dark shirt and he hefted the sawed-off shotgun he was holding like a man who'd love to be given an excuse to use it.

'All right,' he said sibilantly. 'Unbuckle the gun belt. Then step away from it.'

Angel did as he was bid. There was no percentage in bucking a man with a riot gun. Without taking his eyes off Angel, Andy scooped the belt and gun up off the ground, and gestured with the shotgun.

'OK,' he said. 'Jest walk on up ahead o' me, nice an' quiet-like.'

'Listen,' Angel said.

'Walk, boy,' Andy said, and prodded him with the shotgun.

Angel shrugged and led the way up the street. People were spilling out of the saloons and the eating houses. They lined the sidewalk, gawking at him as he went by, then at the group of men headed by the marshal, whose two helpers were carrying the wounded man on a makeshift stretcher. 'Who got shot?' they shouted.

'What the hell happened down there, Ray?' they called.

'Who's the big feller, Andy?' they yelled.

The marshal ignored them. He walked up the center of the littered street looking neither to the right nor to the left, and turned into the frame shack that was his office. Andy brought in Angel, and lifted his right buttock onto a corner of the marshal's desk, covering the prisoner with the shotgun in a hostile, angry attitude. The marshal slid into his chair and regarded the prisoner with disfavor.

'All right,' he said. 'Let's hear your story.'

'No story,' Angel said. 'Marshal—?'

'Name's Compton, son,' the marshal said. He was not a young man, and he had the self-satisfied look of a small businessman who has done rather well for himself in an unspectacular way. Angel put his age at around fifty, and understood now the marshal's nervous tension out in the street. Probably never expected to have to pull a gun in anger, he thought, and it came as a shock to him when he had to.

'I was just riding in,' he told the lawman. 'I got level with the alley down the street there, and the next thing I knew my horse was gut-shot and three men were trying to kill me.'

'For no particular reason, of course,' Compton said heavily. 'Just didn't like the way you sat in the saddle, I suppose?'

'Look, Marshal,' Angel said patiently, 'I was never here before in my life. Don't know a soul in town. Listen, how about letting me see the wounded man. Maybe he can throw some light on this.'

'Ain't likely,' Compton said. 'He croaked halfway up the street an' no wonder – you put three bullets through his belly.'

'I was trying to stay alive,' Angel said reasonably. 'Can I see him?'

'No hurry,' Compton said. 'He ain't going no place.'

'No,' Angel said, sensing what was coming. 'But I am.'

'As to that,' Compton said, 'we'll see. First you answer a few o' my questions.'

He looked up from beneath his heavy eyebrows and put an edge on his voice. 'An' answer me straight, boy,' he added. 'I been known to keep fellers who lied to me locked up months at a time.'

The deputy, Andy, sniggered.

'Months at a time, boy,' he parroted.

Angel felt his temper surge and checked it before it showed. A show of temper was just what Compton wanted, so he could show his authority, kick his prisoner into the hoosegow, and forget him until he was prepared to eat dirt. No one knew Angel was here, so no one would come looking for him if he got himself thrown into Canon City's undoubtedly unpleasant jail. He could rot in this wide spot in the road while Falco and his men got clear out of Colorado Territory. Easy, he told himself, take it easy.

'Name?' Compton asked, licking on the stub of a pencil.

'Frank Angel,' Angel replied. He had already set his mind to work on the problem of who had tried to assassinate him. The only obvious answer was Falco and his men. Except for one thing: there was no way they could have known he was coming to Canon City. Unless. . . .

'You say Angel?' Compton said, incredulously.

'Holy shee-hit!' Andy added.

'Angel,' the prisoner repeated. 'Frank Angel. And I've heard all the jokes about wings and haloes and heaven, Marshal.'

'Angel,' Compton repeated. 'Well, I'll be damned.'

Angel's attention wasn't even on him; the prisoner was still busy on the problem he had set himself. There was just one way Falco and his men could have known he was coming. And if it was true. . . .

'Marshal,' he said, urgency in his voice now. 'Is there a telegraph office in town?'

'Why, sure thing,' Compton said, the sarcasm larding his tone. 'Not to mention the Turkish baths an' the Japanese massoosies an' them two duchesses workin' in the cathouse.'

'Haw, haw, haw,' Andy said, without an ounce of humor in his voice.

'Listen, Marshal, I'm serious,' Angel said.

'Me, too, sonny,' Compton said. 'Now what part o' the country you from? You sure as hell ain't from 'round here.'

'Washington,' Angel said. Without thinking he reached for the secret pocket in his belt and as he did so Andy came off the corner of the desk in a fast, ugly movement, jamming the wicked double mouth of the shotgun into Angel's belly hard enough to make his teeth click.

'You better take it right easy, sonny,' Compton said, leaning back in his chair. 'Or Andy thar's liable to blow you forty ways to Sunday.'

'Bet your ass!' hissed the deputy.

'Listen,' Angel said, looking past Andy at the marshal. 'In my belt is a badge. I want to show it to you.'

'Let him get his badge, Andy,' the marshal said. Reluctantly, the deputy eased back on the pressure, and Angel took out the silver badge. It made a bright, ringing sound as he tossed it on to the marshal's desk. Compton looked at the screaming eagle, the circular seal with the words Department of Justice, and pushed it away with one finger, unimpressed.

'You could've stole that,' he pointed out.

'All right,' Angel said. This time he brought out his Special Commission and unfolded it, spreading it out flat on the desk beneath the oil lamp where the marshal could see what it said.

Know all men by these presents that Frank Warren Angel, holding the office of special investigator, Department of Justice, is empowered by the president of the United States to act for and represent the attorney general in all matters of concern to his department.

*In his capacity, the aforesaid Frank Warren Angel may take
any action that he sees fit to maintain civil or military law
and order, this to include where necessary the convening of
grand juries, the holding of special courts, the empanelment
of juries, the subpoena of witnesses and the conducting of
general courts-martial. He is also empowered to supervene
the authority of any officer of the law, civil, or military,
territorial or federal, where he so desires. All United States
citizens, all officers of the law both federal and territorial are
requested and required to render him such assistance and
support as he may demand in the performance of his duties.*

It was signed by the president of the United States, and
countersigned by his attorney general. The marshal
sighed as he finished reading it.

'Andy,' he said. 'Put that damned gun away.'

He got up and came around his desk, his hands spread
in a placating gesture.

'I'm sorry, Mr Angel,' he said. 'What do you want me to
do?'

'Hey,' Andy said. 'What the hell is this?'

'Shut your mouth, Andy,' Compton said, pleasantly.
Andy shut his face like a trap, his ratty eyes burning with
the fury behind them.

'The dead man,' Angel said. 'I want to take a look at
him. Then I need a horse – the best you can lay your hands
on.'

'That all?'

'If I think of anything, I'll let you know,' Angel said. He
gestured for Compton to precede him out of the office,
ignoring the glowering eyes of the deputy and wondering
what he had done to provoke the man's hatred. They
crossed the street to a white-painted frame shack with a

low picket fence around a small kitchen garden in front of it. There was a light over the porch and Angel waited as the marshal knocked on the door. It was opened by a gray-haired, cadaverous-looking man with eyes that looked as if they had witnessed every conceivable human aberration and still found compassion possible. The deep-set eyes moved from the marshal's face to Angel's and back again.

'Ray,' the man said. 'What can I do for you?'

'Like to take a look at that dead man, Doc,' Compton said. 'This here's Mister Frank Angel. He's from the Department of Justice in Washington. Angel, this is Doc Napier.'

'Hi, Doc,' Angel said softly.

'Hi yourself,' Napier said, looking more closely at him. 'Aren't you the one who—?'

'He is,' Compton said, tersely, and led the way into the hallway. There were two green-painted doors on both sides of the narrow passage, and the marshal opened the first one on the left. Inside it was the unadorned room which Napier used for a surgery. Angel smelled the fish-honey taint of death, and the sharper stink of formaldehyde. On a plain plank table lay the dead man, already stripped naked by the doctor for his examination. The three bullet wounds in the man's belly looked as if someone had spilled violet ink on his skin.

'Davy Livermoor,' Angel said softly. 'He'll steal no more herd money.'

'How's that?' Compton asked, sharply.

'His name's Davy Livermoor,' Angel said. 'He's wanted down Fort Worth way for stealing the price of a herd he took up to Sedalia. Likely there'll be a reward out for him.'

'Which no doubt you'll be claimin',' sneered Compton. He faltered as Angel turned and just looked levelly at him for a long moment.

'I don't have the time,' Angel said softly. 'How about the horse as a trade.'

'Well, as to that,' Compton said. 'You got a deal.'

He hurried out of Napier's house, and Angel watched as the doctor replaced the sheet over the still form of Davy Livermoor.

'You have to forgive Ray, Mr Angel,' Napier said. 'He's what you would call a man who stoops to every challenge.' There was no condescension in his voice, just a soft sadness at all folly.

'Forget it, Doc,' Angel said. 'Life's too short to take offense at that kind of opacity. Listen, I need some information about that one's sidekicks.' He jerked his chin toward the surgery. 'Where's my best place to get it?'

'Over at the Eldorado,' Napier told him. 'That's our local bull pen. Or ask Andy Wheatcroft, Ray's deputy. There isn't much goes on in town he doesn't know about.'

'I may do that,' Angel said, not commenting on Compton's deputy who, if his expression when last Angel saw him had been anything to go by, wouldn't have given Frank Angel typhus without making him pay for it.

'Tell Compton where I am, will you?'

He shook hands with the doctor and walked out into the street. Canon City was back to dull normality. One or two horsemen moving up the street. The sound of a badly-tuned piano being played in the saloon. A woman laughing softly somewhere in the darkness. He got to the Eldorado and pushed in through the batwings. It was a big square place, one room with a bar down the right hand side. On the left were some tables and chairs, and at the back of the room there was a chuckaluck wheel and a faro layout. The place was half-empty, maybe ten or fifteen men sitting around, three more at the bar. One of them, his boot heel hooked on the brass rail, was Compton's deputy Andy Wheatcroft.

'Beer,' he told the bartender, 'and maybe you could give me some information.'

'Beer, coming up,' the bartender said. He was a little fellow with pudgy hands and black, button-bright eyes. His hair was pasted in greasy strands across the balding dome of his head, and his bushy sideburns were heavily pomaded. He smelled, Angel thought, like Saturday night at the whorehouse in Mexico City. 'As to information,' the bartender continued, 'that's another thing again.'

'You heard about the fracas outside,' Angel said. It wasn't a question. The bartender looked uneasily toward Andy Wheatcroft. The deputy wasn't even looking in his direction, but he was listening to what was said.

'Sure,' the bartender nodded. 'Sure. Who didn't?'

'You know the man who got killed?' Angel asked. 'Ever see him?'

'I don't know who got killed,' the bartender said. 'I never seen it.'

'He was one of a group who were in here, yesterday, maybe even today,' Angel said. 'One of them was a kid, tow-headed. Pale blue shirt and tight-fitting fawn pants. You'd remember him. Another was a German. Scarred face, like he'd been in a knife fight. Cropped hair. You recall them?'

The bartender nodded nervously, like a bird pecking up crumbs.

'Sure, sure,' he said. 'Them fellers. Who could forget?'

'When were they in here?'

'Oh, a couple of times,' the bartender said. 'They were in here yesterday, the day before that. You know.'

'I don't suppose,' Angel said, 'you heard them say anything about where they might be heading?'

'Nope,' the bartender said, shaking his head. 'Nothing.' He looked very, very nervous and Angel couldn't figure out why.

'What do I owe you?' he asked.

'Twenty-five cents for the beer,' the man said. And then, all in a rush, as though afraid to speak the words but knowing he must, 'An' twenty-five dollars for the information.'

Angel just looked at the perspiring little man and then he laughed. 'You're kidding,' he said, softly.

'No,' the bartender said defiantly. 'Twenty-five dollars!'

'Hey,' Angel said. 'What is this?'

'Nothing,' the bartender said. 'You give me my money. I don't want any trouble with you.'

'An' you ain't gonna have none, Harry,' said a familiar voice. Angel turned slowly to see Andy Wheatcroft standing at his elbow and then he understood. The deputy had his hand wrapped around the butt of his holstered sixgun. It had a staghorn handle. They always did, Angel thought. He let a slow sigh escape his lips.

'What is this, Wheatcroft?' he asked.

'Nothin' serious, little Angel,' the deputy grinned. 'Unless you're figurin' on not payin' your bill. In which case, you got trouble.'

'Listen,' Angel said, reasonably. 'There's no call for this.'

'I'm makin' call,' Andy said. 'I ain't taken to you at all, little Angel.'

'Look,' Angel said, trying one more time. 'I'll pay for the beer. Then I'll be on my way. Nobody's got to get hurt. What do you say?'

'Crawlin' already, little Angel?' Wheatcroft sneered.

'Makes no odds. You're on your way all right. It's up to you whether you go vertical or horizontal.'

Angel shook his head sadly. There were men like Andy Wheatcroft in every dirty little trail town in the West. They were little men, and they lived on a steady diet of envy and hate. Depending on the town, they were usually pimps, gamblers, or hustlers. Often they were also sadistic back-shooters and far too often they were lawmen. Once in awhile one of them got weeded out by pushing his brand of justice too hard with the wrong man, but more often they stayed in their own bright little pool of poison, eating away at what they were sworn to uphold, every bite they took poisoning not just their own little piece of the law, but every man's opinion of it. There was no cure for them: they had to be stepped on like bugs.

Nobody saw his hand move.

One moment he was standing, his attitude placating, back to the bar and leaning slightly away from the glaring face of the deputy. The next, his hand stabbed forward, the knuckles of the first three fingers held so that they formed a terrible weapon. That right hand moved little more than eighteen inches and struck the deputy just above the breastbone, its awful force paralyzing the man. Wheatcroft's eyes bulged out and his face turned purple as his astonished system struggled to obey the frantic commands of the brain to get oxygen pumped out by the heart literally stunned by the vicious blow. Wheatcroft's knees sagged, and his mouth dropped open like a gutted shark. He made a horrid gargling noise, and his right hand twitched as he tried to make it pull the staghorn-butted sixgun from the holster.

'Tut, tut,' Angel said, seeing the movement.

That same deadly right hand flickered down to the

holstered gun at his side, and came up and out and around in a movement that defeated sight. The barrel of the Colt hit Wheatcroft just above the left ear and he went down in a jarring crash of flailing limbs that made the bottles and glasses jingle on the shelves behind the bar. Nobody moved.

There was a silence that could have been sliced and sold. The terrible suddenness of Angel's action, the callous indifference of the man who had unleashed it were bizarre and chilling and no one wanted to trigger such violence again. And now Angel, knowing to the centimeter the effect of what he had done, turned slowly to face the bartender.

Harry's face had turned as gray as the collar of his once-white shirt.

'Uh,' he said. 'Unh.'

'How was that, Harry?' Angel said, pleasantly. 'What did you say?'

'Honest, mister,' the man stuttered. 'I was. Just. Just josh – kidding, mister. I wasn't serious, honest.'

'Sure, Harry,' Angel said.

'No, listen, it's true, they never said nothin' the whole time, except maybe have a drink, like that,' Harry blurted. 'It's the truth, mister.'

'Oh, I believe you, Harry,' Angel said, every syllable declaring flatly that if Harry had told him the date, he'd have checked it with a calendar.

Harry looked about him piteously for help that he knew he had no right to hope for and that was damned well not about to arrive. He racked his brain for something to tell this smiling man, who had so casually crushed Andy Wheatcroft. Before he could speak, Angel interrupted his thoughts.

'Who put you up to that twenty-five dollars business, Harry?' Angel asked, his voice as soft as ever.

'Uh,' Harry said, hesitating until Angel leaned slightly forward on the bar. Then he made a fast decision. Andy Wheatcroft might give him some stick later, but that would be later. This softspoken stranger would give him hell now, and he wasn't about to take the chance. 'He – Andy, there. He told me to do it.'

'You know why?'

'No idea,' Harry said, truthfully. 'Looked to me like he just wanted some excuse to quarrel with you.'

'Pretty pointless,' Angel mused.

'I think it was mebbe on account o' them fellers you was askin' about,' Harry said. 'Andy there, he spent quite a lot o' time with them.'

'Did he now?' Angel said, softly.

Harry the bartender looked pleased; as if he personally had solved all Angel's problems for him. In fact, Harry didn't give a hoot in hell who solved Angel's problems for him, just so long as Angel went out of the saloon pronto and never came back into it again ever.

'Harry,' Angel said. 'Let me have a jug of water, will you?'

Harry hastened to oblige, and watched fascinated as Frank Angel poured the water, without haste, over the head of the sprawled deputy, who was breathing stertorously, like a man under water. Andy Wheatcroft spluttered, coughed, retched, rolling his head to one side and then another to try to escape the cascading water. His eyes came open, and as they did, Frank Angel got hold of the deputy's shirt front and hauled him to his feet. He pushed Wheatcroft backward into a bentwood chair at a vacant table and lifted the man's chin with his right hand so that

Wheatcroft's eyes were level with his own.

'Andy,' he said. 'I want to ask you about your friends.'

'Go crap in your hat!' Wheatcroft spat venomously.

His words brought another stillness in the saloon. The onlookers held their breath as Angel shook his head sadly, like a schoolteacher let down by a favorite pupil.

'Let me ask you again,' he said. He was holding Wheatcroft's shoulder, almost negligently, and no one really saw the way his fingers moved on the deep nervous center above the big levator scapulae muscles but Wheatcroft's head went back, and his eyes widened with the shocking pain. His face went a sick gray but before he screeched his pain, Angel released the pressure.

'Where did they go, Andy?' he asked, quite pleasantly.

'Fuck you!' Wheatcroft hissed.

'If I do this really hard, it'll probably paralyze your left arm for a couple of months, Andy,' Angel said, reminding Wheatcroft of the pain by increasing the pressure on the nervous system again.

'Aaaah,' Wheatcroft said.

'Quite,' Angel remarked. Relentlessly, he increased the pressure. The bartender and the other men in the room looked at the tableau with open mouths, unable to figure why Wheatcroft was the color of a gaffed catfish.

'Up the river!' Wheatcroft said.

'Up the river? Which river?'

'The Arkansas. They said it was a long pull all the way up the Arkansas. That's all. For God's sake, Angel, that's all they said!'

Angel released his grip, thinking about what Wheatcroft had just said. Up the Arkansas meant, in real terms, that Falco and his men were turning north, heading back up into the mountains. Durango lay to the south and west, which meant that Durango had been a blind. But why north? North lay only the mining camps, Buena Vista and Leadville and the Chalk Creek diggings. Beyond them the high passes that lay ten thousand feet up at the crest of the Continental Divide. Beyond that again, more camps, and then the endless tumble of the mountains, the cordillera, the central spine of the country. If they bore west, they faced five hundred miles of nothing, ending in the City of the Saints, Salt Lake. They wouldn't be heading for the Mormon capital, no way. Which left only one place they could be going – Denver.

'Of course,' he said, softly, beginning to see it all now.

Andy Wheatcroft stared up at him, the weak, Cupid-bow mouth loose with the reaction to pain. If his eyes could have killed, Angel would have dropped dead at the deputy's feet.

'Wheatcroft,' Angel said, ignoring the venom in then man's gaze. 'I'm serving you notice. You're not cut out for the law. My advice to you would be to hand in your badge, as soon as you can. You keep the wrong kind of company. *Sabe?*'

Wheatcroft nodded, the hatred still burning in back of his eyes.

'Do it right soon,' Angel told him softly. 'Or I'll come looking for you. You know what I mean?'

Again Wheatcroft nodded, but the soft whisper of death in Angel's voice had driven all the fury from his eyes, replacing it with naked fear.

Just then, Marshal Compton came in through the batwing doors, and Harry the bartender let out a sigh of relief they could probably hear in Colorado Springs. Compton took in the whole scene in one swift glance: the silent room, the stock-still spectators, the gray-faced figure of his deputy in the bentwood chair, and Frank Angel standing over him. Harry's sweaty face and enormous gasp of relief completed the story, and he walked across the silent saloon to where Angel stood.

'The horse is outside,' he said, levelly. 'I'd like for you to be on it and on your way. Right soon.' He smiled at Angel's nod of acquiescence and jerked a thumb at Andy Wheatcroft.

'What happened to him?'

'He bumped into something,' Angel said. 'Hard.'

'Bound to happen, sooner or later,' Compton said, unfeelingly. He looked at Angel and raised his eyebrows, and Angel nodded. He led the way across the saloon and out into the street. The horse was standing hipshot at the hitching rail, a chunky bay gelding. Its legs were in good shape, mouth firm, chest strong. About five years old, Angel judged from the animal's mouth, and not hard used. It would be as good a horse as he had any right to hope for in a town like Canon City.

'Nice animal,' he said, as he swung into the saddle. 'Thanks.'

'No thanks necessary,' Compton said. 'In fact, I oughta thank you.'

'For what?'

'Not killin' Andy Wheatcroft.'

Angel neckreined the bay around, pointing him up the street. Even though it was already dark, he wanted to get as far away from Canon City as he could. It was the kind of place whose smell stuck to your clothes.

'It wasn't because he didn't need killing,' he said, and put the horse into a trot. He didn't look back. There wasn't a damned thing to look back for.

NINE

Chris Falco was in a bind.

The whole plan had been hung on their killing Angel in Canon City. The place was way off the beaten track, the marshal inadequate at best, and they had bought themselves an 'in' with the deputy as easy as falling down. By the time Angel's death had been reported or discovered, they would have been long gone. It was for this that Willowfield had so obligingly offered himself as bait – to bring any pursuer out into the open where he could be dealt with. Then Falco and the rest would double back through the mountains to Denver, ambush the escort taking the fat man back east, and release him so they could go dig up the money. There was one additional facet to the plan, added by Falco, that Willowfield didn't know about yet: Falco intended to kill him.

Now, however, he was in a bind: and he was going to have to improvise. Angel had to be taken care of, somehow, and not just to secure their backtrail. The man's reactions had been incredible, unexpected. He had not only wasted Davy Livermoor, but one of his bullets had torn a wicked hole through the thigh of Hank Kuden. Falco looked over his shoulder. Kuden wasn't riding ramrod-straight like he usually did. His lips were clamped together in a bloodless line against the pain he must be feeling. Falco knew that with the hard mountain riding ahead of them, Kuden was going to come off his horse sooner or later. And when it happened, the German would never get back on again.

'Hold up,' he called. 'Hank, come up here!'

The others reined in their horses. They were already high up on the flanks of Mount Antero, and the chill was insidious, despite their bundled clothing. Their breath steamed in the night air as they bunched around their leader and watched as Kuden walked his horse up alongside Falco's. They saw the effort he made to look good, pulling his back straight, lifting his chin.

'How is it?' Falco asked, straight out.

'All right,' Kuden said. 'Not good. But I can manage.' He said it 'manitch.'

'Hank, you're lying.'

'Yes. I am lying,' Kuden flared. 'You vant truth? I tell it you. Is terrible. It stinks. It hurt like hell. Does dot make you feel bedder?'

'In a way,' Falco said, softly. 'In a way.'

Kuden just looked at him; he had the expression of a soldier who knows he's going to get an order he cannot obey.

'I want you to lay back,' Falco said. 'Try and take Angel out. Then go back to Canon City, get the doc to look at your leg.'

'No,' Kuden said. 'I go forward.'

'Listen,' Falco said urgently. 'You're bogging us down, Hank. The speed we're moving, that Fed will be up with us tomorrow. You keep riding, we're going to be even worse off.'

'Why we not all wait for this man, and kill him?'

88

'Hank,' Falco said, with one of those 'surely you know better' looks. 'We got a deadline, remember? We've got to get to Fort Morgan before the colonel. And we're already behind schedule.'

'Ach, yes,' Kuden said. 'I forget that.'

'You'll do it?'

'If I do it, how I get my share of the money?' Kuden asked.

'Shit, that's easy, Hank,' Falco said, putting a false warmth into his voice. 'Rent a buggy in Canon City, drive over to Colorado Springs. Take the train up to Cheyenne. Be there on the fifteenth, an' I'll meet you. Bring you your share. How's that?'

'Good,' Kuden nodded. 'Logical. You will do this?'

'Hank!' Falco said, injecting an injured tone into his voice. 'You know you can rely on me. Don't you?'

'*Ja*,' Kuden said, slowly. 'I guess so. I guess I can.'

'All right, then,' Falco said. 'You'll do it?'

Kuden looked at them all. The lack of interest on their faces was total. They didn't give a damn whether he lived or died. If he took Angel, then that would be fine, a benefit. If not, *es spielt keine Rolle*, one less to share the money with. He cursed his own bad luck, the chance shot that had crippled him. He had a good reason to kill Frank Angel, anyway. He might as well do it. If he tried to keep up with them, he'd probably pass out soon. And then they'd either kill him themselves, or leave him to freeze or starve to death in the mountains. At least this way, he could come out of it alive. And get to Cheyenne to meet Falco. Yes, he told himself. It was as good a way as any.

'I do it,' he said.

'Fine,' Falco said, enthusiastically. 'You got plenty of ammo?'

Kuden tapped the ammunition pouch on the cantle of the saddle.

'Hank,' Gil Curtis said. 'You're in no shape to get close in. Use the rifle.'

'Good, good idea,' Kuden nodded. 'I do it.'

'OK, then,' Falco said, pulling his horse around. 'Let's move out. We got a long way to go. Hank – we'll see you in Cheyenne!' In a pig's eye, he added, mentally.

Kuden raised his hand in farewell salute as Falco kicked his horse into a canter to catch up with the others, who were already moving fast up the trail. Don't you worry, Falco, I'll be there. If I got to crawl every inch of the way. And if you doublecross me I'll stay on your backtrail for as long as it takes to find you and cut your throat, Kuden thought. He cocked back his head and looked at the sky. Off over the black hulk of the mountains he thought he could detect a faint thinning of the blackness. He checked his pocket watch. Four o'clock. He had a couple of hours to get ready before it was light. He started looking for a good place from which to kill Angel.

By dawn, Angel was saddled up and on the move.

He had camped overnight in the lee of a huge rock overhang crowned with small, closely set pine and thin silver birch. Beneath the overhang, the blown fall leaves were still dry and he made a comfortable mattress out of them. He picketed the horse where it could be seen and built a fire. The night chill was biting, and he knew that the dampness he could feel in the air would soon be translated into snow on the high peaks. Soon, it would be snowing even at this height, and when it snowed up here, it snowed in earnest: five feet overnight was normal. Ten, fifteen, twenty feet wasn't remarkable. He didn't want to be caught in the open, hostile wilderness if the weather broke. So far October had been mild, its winds soft even this high. He knew he'd have to buy some heavier clothing when he got to Buena Vista. He figured it was about ten miles north.

Off to his left now was a sheer-sided canyon, its north side the lower reaches of Mount Princeton, its southern Mount Antero. The mountains soared away up above the white chalk cliffs that bordered a creek which chattered beneath the deeply shadowed cliffs on its way to merge with the Arkansas, close to whose banks he was riding now. The trail was wide, and led through stands of aspen and pine that broke up in grassy clearings that sloped down to the purling river. Off to his right, the foothills of the mountains of South Park began, and the towering peaks made his progress seem painfully slow.

A flicker of movement caught his eye up on the crags. He saw it was an eagle, which spread its wings and soared into the cloudless sky. It flew in a long straight line from his right, coming lower as it crossed his path toward the canyon on the left. Then, as he watched, it made a sharp, veering turn away, the movement of the wide, strong wings accelerating in steady beats. Angel watched it go, the frown of concentration deepening between his brows. Easing back against the cantle of the saddle, he braced his legs against the stirrups and let his eyes move carefully across the barren rocks frowning down upon the trail. Nothing moved. He looked for nothing, letting his own fine eyesight do the work. He knew that anything which moved would catch his eyes as long as they weren't focused on anything in particular. He saw nothing, and knew he was going to have to rely on the horse. He got himself ready to move and gigged the horse forward, poised but not tense. When the horse pricked up his ears, he went over the far side, hearing the angry zzzzizzz of the slug a fraction of a second before the hard flat clap of a Winchester echoed off the faceless rocks. Up to the left, he thought as he rolled in the dew-wet grass. The horse had shied at his sudden movement and the sound of the shot, but he had thrown the reins forward, and the animal came to a stop, the reins trailing, settling to placidly crop the thin grass. Angel lay where he had fallen, face down, legs akimbo, doing his best to look dead. He knew it would be a long wait now, the killer would take no chances, might not even come down to make sure. He had heard no sound of a horse moving away, but that didn't mean one hadn't. He had to stay down and wait. There was no way he could get to a man with a rifle hidden behind rocks. He had to try to make the man come to him and he withdrew into himself, the way that the Korean, Kee Lai, had taught him during the training sessions in the echoing gymnasium that the Justice Department shared: 'The mind and the body are one. Both produce life-energies. Both can be controlled as one. Control the mind first. Then control the body. And at last you will control both as one. Only then can you summon all of yourself, all of your strength and mind and energy, into one place, one instant, and use it as one. You can be, you will be, more than other men if you can learn this. Learn, learn, learn. . . .'

In his mind's eye, he could see his own sprawled body and the geography of the place in which he had fallen as clearly as if he were the eagle whose avoiding action had saved his life. He lay on sloping grass-covered ground that fell away from the side of the trail toward the swirling river. There were trees perhaps twenty feet away from his head, more eighty or ninety feet downstream. He lay with his leg slightly bent, right knee higher. Left hand palm down near his head, arm bent; right arm almost straight, palm up, not far from the right knee. He disciplined his breathing so that it became shallow, shallower, almost imperceptible. And then he waited. He attempted no assessment of time, concentrating upon absolutely nothing, every sense acutely tuned. He heard the birds moving overhead, or singing in the darkness of the woods. He heard the softness of the river moving over sliding pebbles, the soughing of the faint breeze that shifted the branches of the trees, the slow inevitable turning of the earth.

A twig snapped.

It wasn't the horse; the horse was downstream of him, contentedly cropping at the grass. So it had to be the hunter who was his prey. He concentrated upon keeping death-still. If the ambusher saw even the movement of Angel's breathing, he might come no closer, but render the *coup de grâce* from six feet away. He tracked the man's movements, following his approach from the slight sounds. He could see the dark figure clearly through the windows of his mind, moving down the long slope away from which the eagle had veered, down through the fringing timber and across the trail – soft slither of leather on stone – then to the edge of the clearing in which Angel lay – soft underfoot crackling of pine needles, tiny squelch of wet leaves. There the man stopped. Angel could hear his heavy, ragged breathing. The man was in poor condition or in pain, he couldn't tell which. He heard the tentative soft swish of movement through the dew-wet grass. It stopped again. Was the man dragging one foot? Almost as if the ambusher was giving off tangible warmth, a field of energy, Angel could sense his very closeness. He knew the man was near enough to touch him now, and steeled himself. The metallic sound of a hammer going back on rifle or pistol would mean that Angel had no time, no chance at all. He heard the man exhale as he bent over the prone body. Kuden put a hand under Angel's shoulder in order to turn him over and in that moment Angel summoned all of himself into one movement. His right hand took the hand grasping his left shoulder and he came up off the ground with the left hand pushing, turning his left shoulder down as his body came up fast and strong, acting as a fulcrum. Kuden went up across Angel's shoulders and then down with a heavy wet thud on the grass. The Winchester cartwheeled out of his hand and he yelled with pain, yet still he rolled like a thrown cat. He was already on his feet and lunging at Angel by the time Angel wheeled upright to face him, giving Angel no chance to get set. Kuden smashed into Angel head down, bowling Angel over backward, pounding his fists into Angel's face. Locked together they thrashed across the grassy clearing, each seeking purchase, breath coming harsh and hard as they fought with strengths almost evenly matched. Finally, Angel got one hand momentarily free and using the edge of his hand like the blade of an ax, chopped backward and upward at Kuden's throat. The German coughed and retched, his eyes bugging as he rose upright as if trying to escape the gagging paralysis of his Adam's apple, and as he did, Angel turned and kicked the man's right leg out from beneath him.

Kuden went down with a screech of agony that sent birds chattering in scolding panic through the silent trees. He lay face down in the flattened grass, his whole body humping over with the pain, and now for the first time, Angel saw the dark wet spread of blood on the man's thigh. Kuden rolled over on his back, his face distorted in a rictus of pain as he tried to get up off the floor. Angel made his decision, and when Kuden was on his knees, Angel clenched the knuckles of his right hand and hit the man with considered strength, just above the point at the back of his neck were there was a V-shaped joint above the second cervical vertebra. Kuden went down face forward in the grass, out like a doused candle. With deft movements, Angel searched and disarmed the unconscious man.

Then he set about seeing what he could do to patch him up. Capture, not kill, the Old Man had said.

'*Leek mein Arsch!*' Kuden snarled.

'Not just now,' Angel said, gently. 'Let's try again. Which route are they taking?'

This time the German just spat and Angel shrugged. Kuden wasn't his top priority, and by and large, his information was likely to be only confirmation of Angel's already formulated estimate. He wondered whether the attorney general realized what he'd required with that 'capture, not kill' edict. After he'd cleaned up the ragged hole in Kuden's thigh as best he could with boiled river water and some iodine, Angel had bound the German's leg firmly with bandage strips made from a spare shirt he found in the man's bedroll. Then he had cut two stout sticks and fashioned a clumsy splint – two reasons for that. One, it was the right thing to do, medically; two, it would prevent Kuden doing anything sudden. Later, Angel had made a travois, rounded up Kuden's horse, strapped the trailing A-shaped litter to its saddle, and led the way up the trail looking for all the world like some Ute moving house. After a couple of hours, he had found what he was looking for: a sheltered cave on the flank of the mountain, not too high for Kuden to get up there. He'd ignored the man's puzzled face on the way up, and ignored him as he built a fire and cooked some food. The cave smelled like a cat's litter: puma had been here, he guessed. Their acrid tang soon dispersed in the smell of the woodsmoke. He gave Kuden something to eat and then told him the bad news. Kuden's answer had been, to say the least of it, uncooperative.

'Kuden,' he said, sadly. 'I'll give you one more chance.'

Kuden said nothing. He turned his head away ostentatiously, staring at the patch of sky above the mountains that could be seen from the entrance to the cave.

Angel sighed. If information kept on being this hard to come by, he was going to end up being some kind of Marquis de Sade. He tried once more. 'Let me put it another way,' he said. 'I'll tell you what I think. Then you tell me whether I'm right or wrong. OK?'

He allowed himself a grin at Kuden's expression; it would be worth talking it out, just to hear what it sounded like. There was always the chance Kuden would react. Not much of a chance, perhaps. But a chance.

'Here's how it happened, Kuden,' Angel said. 'Near as I can figure. Your boss Willowfield knew nobody could derail a train, rip off a quarter of a million dollars, kill Federal agents, and not have the law on his backtrail before you could say "holdup." Maybe he was surprised I turned up so quick – there wasn't any way he could have known I'd survived the train wreck – but it made no difference to the plan. He told Falco and the rest of you to hole up and wait for the word. As soon as the law turned up, he'd sit there and be taken like a pigeon, quiet as a mouse. Tell the law where Falco and the rest of you were heading.

And let whoever it was ride straight into your guns. By the time anyone got on your trail again, you'd be long gone.'

'Very clever, Mister Angel,' the German sneered.

'I went to college,' Angel said. Kuden spat in the fire, his face contemptuous. 'However, the plan to blow me up didn't work. So I killed Livermoor and put a hole in your leg. Falco had to do some improvising. And you were it. What did he tell you – hang back, kill me, and he'd meet up with you someplace?'

He nodded as he saw Kuden's look.

'And you fell for it,' he sneered. 'Falco couldn't lose, could he? You killed me, he was home free. I cut you down, ditto. He probably had you down as a write-off anyway, with that leg.'

Kuden's face was now a study in bottled rage, but he still disciplined himself not to rise to the baiting.

'So – the big question. I'd say Falco's on his way back to Denver, where the idea is to spring the fat man some-where. The only thing I don't know is which route they're taking. And where they plan to attack the escort and spring Willowfield.'

Kuden repeated his earlier invitation, putting the whole conversation back to square one. Angel regarded his pris-oner sadly, putting onto his face the exasperated expres-sion of a teacher with a clever child who won't try.

'Ah, well,' he said at last. 'I ought to have known you'd want to do it the hard way.'

For the first time, he caught the alarm in Kuden's eyes. It was quickly concealed, but it was there. Angel unrolled Kuden's bedroll on the floor of the cave, and told him to lie on it, face up.

'What for?' Kuden demanded.

'Do it!' Angel snapped, emphasizing the command by

pulling out his sixgun and jamming it against Kuden's chin, forcing the German's head back.

The man jumped visibly when Angel cocked the gun, and shifted himself quickly to the bedroll, where he lay, glaring up at his tormentor.

'Comfortable?' Angel said. 'Then we'll begin.'

He tipped Kuden's ammunition pouch upside down, and twenty or so .44/40 cartridges fell to the floor, gleaming dully in the flickering firelight. One by one, Angel extracted the leaden bullets from the brass cases, until he had a line of six beheaded cartridges. He stood them in a line on a thin shelf of rock on the cave wall. Then he emptied three of them, with measured movements, so that there was a thick line of gunpowder perhaps four inches long a foot away from Kuden's head but well within the man's line of vision. Then he struck a match and lit one end of the line of powder. It burned with a fizzing, smoking *buwwwwwwwffff.* and Kuden coughed as the fumes caught at his throat. He looked at Angel as if Angel had gone insane.

'So?' he said defiantly.

'So,' Angel replied. 'We begin.'

He bent down and started to unbutton Kuden's shirt, peeling it back so that the man's naked belly and chest were exposed. Then he unbuckled the German's heavy belt, unfastened his pants, pulling them down. Kuden cursed and struggled, but with his arms and feet as neatly bound as they were, there was little he could do to protest. Now Frank Angel picked up the three cartridges from the rock shelf and Kuden's eyes went round with realization. Angel sprinkled the same kind of thick line of powder from the man's navel to his genitals and then stood back. He took the matches from his pocket.

'*Nein, nein!*' Kuden shrieked, '*Nein, nein, nein!*'

He arched his back, thrashing around, rolling his body to try to dislodge the powder, but his own sweat kept most of it where it had been sprinkled. Then he subsided in cold gut-wrenched fear as Angel snapped a match alight with his thumbnail. Kuden looked up. There wasn't any hint of compassion in Angel's face. It looked as if it had been carved from stone.

'Wait,' Kuden said, his nerve snapping visibly. 'God, wait!'

'Time's up, Kuden,' Angel snapped. 'Sing. Or fry.' His tone made it abundantly clear that he didn't give a good wholesome goddamn which one Kuden chose.

'All right,' the German sobbed. 'All right.'

'Talk,' Angel said, relentlessly.

Kuden talked.

TEN

Buena Vista was little more than a serried double row of scattered shacks interspersed with the occasional stone building paralleling a wide, muddy street that rose sharply toward the north. It hardly lived up to its name. The sidewalks and the street itself were crowded, and outside every store great bundles of washpans, shovels, picks, ropes, and other necessaries of the mining life rattled like dented cowbells in the soft afternoon breeze. Over the whole place hung the suppressed clamor of a dozen different accents and the indefinable hum, the almost tangible fever, that is never very far from a gold camp.

Up every canyon, along every dribbling creek and runoff that fed the Arkansas, otherwise sane men grubbed in the filthy mud for as many hours a day as there was light, more than happy if those backbreaking hours yielded them an ounce of glinting particles of worthless metal – but worthless metal for which men would willingly kill, gladly cheat, happily lie, cheerfully steal, recklessly die. And if those same backbreaking hours yielded them nothing but rotted boots and rheumatic limbs, why, they buckled to and grinned and bore it, and got down to the same job again the next day, dreaming, as they all dreamed of The Big Strike. They sustained the bleakness of their everyday lives with legends – legends in which Striking It Heavy was the happy ending, legends born in a millrace on the south fork of the American River in California, risen again a hundred times in different forms in Arizona and New Mexico and Utah and Nevada and right here in Colorado. The legends survived defeat, despair, disappointment. Someone, somewhere was going to Strike It Heavy sometime. Nobody ever remembered that James Marshall never made a cent out of the gold field he discovered. Men who were not bitten by the gold lust never understood it.

Angel found the office of the town marshal at the northern end of the town, a simple frame cabin with a shingle outside that proclaimed its function. He led Kuden in, and the German stood sullenly behind him, head down as the marshal, a short, rotund man of perhaps fifty, got up from behind a littered rolltop desk, pushed the swing door in the low railing which divided the room in half, and came forward with an inquiring look on his face.

'Well, boys,' he said, 'What's your trouble?'

'No trouble, Marshal,' Angel said. The marshal's handshake was firm, and belied his apparently soft appearance. Angel never made the mistake of equating the fact of a man's stoutness with sloppiness or flabbiness: one of the toughest fist fights he'd ever been in his life was with a short, tubby man who'd worn steel-rimmed spectacles and who had fought with a ferocity and strength that was all the more effective because it had been so unexpected. This marshal could well be another such, he thought: policing a town as tough as Buena Vista was likely to be on a Saturday night, even though the real tide of violence had now swept on to newer, rawer camps, would not be a cakewalk. He gave his name to the lawman, and showed him his identification.

'Department of Justice, is it?' the marshal said. 'Well now.'

He looked at Kuden, who was looking at Frank Angel, with a new light in his eyes.

'Well, bucko,' the marshal said to Kuden. 'You got mixed up with the right bunch this time, didn't you?' He turned to give Angel back the badge and the commission. 'My name's Hedley,' he announced. 'Gwyn Hedley.'

'From Wales?' Angel guessed.

'Originally,' Hedley admitted.

'You been up here long?'

'Long enough, boyo,' Hedley said. 'Long enough. Now, what do you need?'

'Two things,' Angel said. 'One, I want this character put away someplace and kept there until he's well enough to travel.'

'No problem,' Hedley said. 'What's number two?'

'I'm looking for three men who probably went through town late last night or very early this morning,' Angel said. 'The names are Chris Falco, Gil Curtis, and Buddy McLennon. Falco's a big man, well-built, with gray hair on both sides of his head that looks like it's been painted on. Curtis is medium height, dark-haired. McLennon's slim, almost girlish-looking. It's just faintly possible they're still in town, but I doubt it.'

'It won't take us long to check,' Hedley said firmly. 'You want to wait here?'

'No,' Angel said. 'If you can take the prisoner off my hands, I might go get a hot meal. I haven't eaten properly for a couple of days.'

'I'll do better than that, boyo,' Hedley said. 'Come with me while I tuck your little baby away safe, and I'll show you a good place to eat. We can check on your three others at the same time.'

'Bueno,' Angel said. 'Where's your hoosegow?'

'Right on down the street, next to the Lucky Strike,' Hedley said. 'You must've passed it as you came on up.'

Angel nodded, remembering the solid-looking stone building on the left hand side of the street. He gave Kuden a shove to get the man started, and Kuden limped out on to the sidewalk. He had no fight left in him: Angel's gunpowder ploy had removed the starch, and he had told his tormentor everything he wanted to know. Kuden had nothing left to fight for, and even less to fight with. They trooped down the hill.

'What's the charge on this one?' Hedley asked on the way.

'Murder, first degree,' Angel said.

'And his name?'

'Kuden, Hans Kuden.' Angel spelled it for the marshal who crossed the street now and banged on the heavy wooden door of the squat stone building next to the saloon. His deputy, a dour-looking individual with a drooping mustache, a slat-thin, stooped body, and a face that looked as if it had never smiled since infancy, opened up with much sliding of bolts and rattling of keys.

'Who you expectin', Ike?' Hedley said. 'Quantrill's raiders?'

'Never know,' Ike said lugubriously. 'No point takin' chances.'

'Brung you a prisoner,' Hedley said, motioning Angel to follow him inside.

'Jim-dandy,' Ike said, with the tone of someone discovering he has just lost his wallet.

'You speak German?' Angel asked Ike. The deputy

looked at him as if Angel had asked whether he made a habit of molesting small girls.

'You what?' he barked.

'Just wondered,' Angel said, and stood back as Ike pushed Kuden none too gently through a heavy steel door and into a corridor, along which were set four barred cells. He swung the door of one of them open, and Kuden slunk in like a whipped dog.

'I'll arrange for an escort to come collect him,' Angel told Hedley. 'In the meanwhile, he could use a doctor to look at his leg.'

'What happened to him?' Hedley asked.

'He got shot,' Angel said, and Hedley let the matter be. It didn't seem like Angel had any intention of discussing the matter further.

'I'll get the doctor to call over and tend to him,' he promised. 'Ike, I'm going to grab a bite to eat.'

'Fine,' Ike said, sliding back into his bentwood chair and picking up his *Police Gazette*.

'I'll be back in about an hour,' Hedley continued. 'Spell you then.'

'Fine,' Ike said, without lifting his eyes from the magazine.

'By the way, I just heard the world's comin' to an end at midnight,' Hedley remarked casually, with a grin at Angel.

'Fine,' Ike said.

They walked back up the street together. Several times, Hedley stopped to talk to people: some miners he met coming out of a saloon, a storekeeper sweeping the dust out of his place on to the sidewalk whence it would blow back in again, a man sitting on a bench outside a cabin. He stopped and asked questions of a trio of spangled saloon girls switching their rumps along the sidewalk on their way to work in the Lucky Strike. They giggled as they answered, their eyes on the tall figure of Frank Angel. By the time they had reached the top of the street, Angel reckoned Hedley had talked with eight or nine separate sets of people. They all treated him with deference, Angel noted. Now they were back almost opposite the marshal's office, and Hedley jerked a thumb at a frame building, one-story, and as long as a barn, upon the apex of whose roof was a sign which read: *Home Cooking. Steaks a specalty. Home Cooking.*

'Place is run by a guy called Home, Bill Home,' Hedley explained. 'We never minded the pun much, but we give him a bad time every now and then about his spelling.'

The place was half-empty. It was still a little early for the crowds who'd fill the place after dark. There was a smell of fresh bread, coffee, food cooking, and the inescapable mining-town smell of sweaty feet. The waitress was a buxom woman with bright red cheeks and an Irish accent.

'We'll have a couple of your best steaks, Maggie,' Hedley said.

'Coffee?'

'You bet.'

'Want the coffee now?'

'Sure.'

'Comin' up,' Maggie said, bustling away.

'Nice kid,' Hedley said, startling Angel for a moment. Maggie was some way past being a kid, but then he realized that Hedley was old enough to call most people kids. Maggie pushed through the swing doors into the kitchen in back. Cooking smells wafted in.

'Now as to your men,' Hedley said. Angel leaned forward.

'They're here?'

'No such luck,' Hedley said. 'They left around mid-morning, far as I can make out.'

'Damn!' Angel ground out. Six or seven hours start would put them already on the far side of Trout Creek Pass, well on the way to South Park. He said as much, but Hedley shook his head.

'Not likely, boyo,' he said. 'I talked to some miners just came down from Fairplay. They tell me it's raining like hell higher up, might even snow before morning. That being the case, I'd say they was probably already hunkered down someplace doing their best not to freeze solid. It's sartin sure they won't be making over four or five miles an hour even if they're on the move. I'd hazard a guess they might make it up to Fairplay, then stick it out there until it's fit to travel.'

'You reckon I might catch up on them?'

'Could be, you set out tomorrow morning with fine weather, you'll make it twice as fast up there as they did.'

Just at that moment, Maggie came bustling up with their coffee, and before they were halfway through the steaming brew, brought their meals. On each plate, completely concealing the 'Willow Pattern' design, was an inch-thick steak, a fried egg sitting on it. At one side of the steak was a heap of pan-browned potatoes and on the other a helping of canned beans. After the manner of men who spend much of their time outdoors, the marshal and his visitor wasted no more time talking, but fell to with a will. Hungry as he was, however, Hedley was still eating when Angel pushed away his emptied plate with a sigh and leaned back in the ladderback chair.

'Peaches or pie?' Maggie said as she picked up the plates.

They both chose pie, and Angel asked the marshal a question.

'Fairplay?' he replied. 'It's up above Trout Creek Pass. Lies at about ten thousand feet, and cold as a witch's tit this time of the year. Used to be a camp up there in '59 called Tarryall. Miners there ran off anyone who tried to join them, so the newcomers told 'em they oughta rechristen the place Graball. They pushed on up the South Platte and found gold in the gravel bars up there. Town just growed up alongside the river. Settled, now. They got a nice little white Presbyterian church, a two-story courthouse made out of red sandstone. You going up there after this Falco?'

'You better believe it,' Angel told him. 'It would be kind of nice to catch up with them in Fairplay.'

'How come?' Hadley wanted to know.

'Well,' Angel said. 'It has a nice ironic ring to it.'

Chris Falco had stayed alive the best part of forty years by always making sure all his bets were coppered. A man who coppered his bets was one who bet on every horse, calculating the odds so that there were precious few ways he could lose – and Falco had learned early in a colorful life that it was the best way to ensure survival. And survival was his strongest suit. He'd come west with his father, an incurable optimist who always believed he was going to find gold where everyone else had already looked, a beat-up, half-starved, rootless old prospector, but as tough as whang leather. Chris Falco had taken every beating the old man gave him – and there were plenty – without a whimper until he was sixteen and grown tall and broad. Then Carter Falco took a switch to his son once too often, and Chris damned near killed him. He lit out fast from his home near Springfield and ended up in St. Louis, Missouri, where he got a job as a bouncer in a Clark Street bordello. The madame had taken a fancy to him, dressed him well, and given him money to spend. She introduced him to some of her more important clients, one of whom was Danny Johnson, a ward boss in the Seventh District. Pretty soon Chris had a well-paid job as Danny's body-guard and enforcer, and Falco did a hell of a job. Nobody ever got charges against him that would stick and on the few occasions he was busted, Danny Johnson put the fix in and Chris was back on the street. Then one day somebody laid for Danny Johnson as he was coming out of the Golden Slipper on the corner of Maple and Divine, blow-ing him up with cool precision, leaving Falco crawling around in a pool of his own blood. The style of the execu-tion left nobody in any doubt about who was behind it, and Falco knew better than to take on the Italians for anything as futile as revenge. He moved across the river, where he had a few connections, heading into Kansas. There were plenty of things for a sharp guy to get into. The herds were coming up from Texas, and there was a demand for men who knew all the tricks Chris had learned. He did some work with the cards, one of the easi-est ways there was to strip marks; hustled a little, doing some pimping when things got slack – anything for a dishonest buck. His business became one of surviving, of being around, waiting for the big one to walk in through the door, fly over the transom, drop out of a pocket. Willowfield saw him and offered him what he wanted on a plate. All he'd ever hoped for was to get next to one big heist, and just as he had always known it would, it walked in through the door. He had no intention of letting it walk out.

Just the same, he mistrusted complicated plans like the one the fat man had cooked up to deal with the law. It relied on too many imponderables, and there was no way of coppering the bets, as he had already found out. This Angel, for instance: nobody had expected anything like him. The kind of law they had expected, not to say counted on, was the kind the U.S. marshals dished out. U.S. marshals were usually fiftyish, slowed-up hangers-on of whatever political machine was in power. They tended to be beer drinkers with hanging guts who had long since grown averse to hard riding in rough back country. When the occasion or the necessity to do so arose, they hired 'deputies' who were usually down-at-heel bounty hunters or would-be gunfighters anxious to carve a notch on their carbine butt. Nobody mourned when a bounty hunter was missing, or some gun nut wound up face down in some nameless gully. That had been the caliber of pursuit they had expected, not a man who could ride straight under the sights of three carbines and not only come out alive but take out two of his ambushers.

Falco had no intention of letting Angel run him to earth. He didn't really figure that Kuden would have a snowball's chance in hell of stopping Angel, and he made his plans on that basis. It came as no surprise at all to him when Curtis galloped into Buena Vista on a lathered horse and confirmed it.

He'd left Curtis on a high bluff overlooking the trail up the canyon of the Arkansas with a pair of good army field-glasses and the best of the horses. He and McLennon pushed on ahead into Buena Vista to get some supplies, rest the horses, maybe grab a couple of quick drinks.

So now, as they headed on up the mountain trail out of Buena Vista, Falco turned the options over in his mind, unhappy with the picture they presented. It was bad enough that Angel was still coming, but worse news that he had taken Kuden prisoner.

That would mean Kuden had spilled, Falco thought. No point hoping otherwise: act on the premise that the worst has happened. That means he knows what Kuden knows, the original plan. He grinned like a wolf. Nobody knew he'd changed that some. Angel would also know the route they planned to take, and he could do one of two things. Change the route, or take the one Kuden would have told Angel about, and then turn that knowledge against Angel. He decided on the latter.

By now, however, he had a healthy respect for Mister Frank Angel, and when he explained his plan to the others, he set up everything so that once more, his bet on survival was coppered.

In Buena Vista, he'd made himself conspicuous, so that a dozen people or more around town would remember him. He'd gone bareheaded so that the men he'd jostled in front of in the store would recall him. He had criticized the quality of the liquor in the Lucky Strike. He had suggested some particularly vile sexual activities to one of the saloon girls. He smiled in remembering that: no way she would forget him. All in all, he laid a trail that an infant would have had trouble missing, knowing that it would bring Angel out after them, hell bent into the flat emptinesses of South Park. The trail led ever upward into the mountains, cresting at Trout Creek. At Trout Creek Pass they would kill Angel.

ELEVEN

When the weather turns bad in the mountains, it does so very fast.

The horse blew great gusts of wind through its nostrils, which were caked with a rim of frost despite the muffler that Angel had wrapped around the animal's head. They moved steadily upward into the rocky wilderness, heading for Trout Creek Pass. It was quite low – only nine and a half thousand feet as compared to some of the others. Up above Idaho Springs way there were passes well over two miles high, and the wind that cut through them blew from the Arctic to the Antarctic with nothing to stop it but one or two mountain peaks.

The preceding night a wind of hurricane force had sprung up. The night had been alive with the sound of shutters banging, corrugated tin roofs blowing off and banging away down the canyon, whirled up and down the heedless rocks by the whipping wind. Later, the wind showed its teeth, and lashed the canyon of the Arkansas with hailstones the size of prairie oysters, smacking against the thin wooden walls of the shacks down the street of Buena Vista like Gatlin gunfire. The muddy street quickly turned to a gloppy morass, which froze like iron as the night advanced, and the temperature dropped like a stone. A moon glared like a baleful eye through the heaving clouds, and beneath it the mountains emerged, shining ghost-white with their mantling of fresh snow, only to be eclipsed by another sudden storm. Angel had sat by the window of the Lucky Strike, where Hedley had fixed for him to rent a room. It was too noisy to sleep, and he watched the incredible struggle of the elements, thinking of the men he was pursuing up there somewhere in the wilderness. Once in the night he heard the long wail of a wolf, driven down from the heights by the cold. For some reason, the sound reminded him of a time he had been in the mountains just before snow, when a lake had glowed an unearthly orange in the strange twilight, yet reflected the mountains above it deep blue. Somewhere around the middle of the night the storm broke, and he slept. He dreamed formless dreams and rose before dawn, still weary.

Up ahead of him now the mountains glittered and waited. The sun was sharp and bright, and the wind was bitingly, bone-achingly cold. The air was brittle and tasted dry, but he wasn't tempted to take the woolen kerchief away from his face. He'd bought it and a heavy plaid blanket coat, together with a pair of seal-skin pants the preceding night. They just about kept the wind off. At this altitude, it could take off a layer of your flesh with less effort than a good skinner with a cut-throat razor.

The road, the vegetation, the trees on back away from the trail all lay under a glittering mantle of fresh powder snow that sparkled like the enchanted garden in a fairy tale, as if someone had sprinkled finely ground diamonds on the snow. There was no real trail visible, but it was easy enough to keep where the trail should be by following the innumerable tiny tracks of gophers and small birds that marched downhill toward the warmer places in the canyon. After an hour, Angel had to dismount and lead the horse, because the snow had balled so badly in its feet that the animal could hardly walk. Using his hunting knife and a heavy stone, he was able to chip most of it away, but he walked the bay for about another half hour before he got on him again.

Imperceptibly, the light changed, became somehow flat. It created a strange phenomenon: the ground ahead and behind seemed to become completely featureless, the rolls and crests and bumps ironed out to a flat and unbroken expanse wherever he looked by the strange bright mountain light. Nothing moved in the entire empty wasteland: no bird, no beast, no man other than himself. The sky above the looming peaks off to the north was turning a dirty fishbelly gray-white, and he felt the wind freshening. The smell of snow was in the air and the bay shivered, as if he could already feel it.

Up ahead was the pass: a narrow aperture between two redstone buttes towering four hundred feet or more on either side. The impenetrable carpet of pine trees lying on both sides of the pass looked like frosted buffalo fur. Here and there on the floor of the pass lay enormous shattered lumps of stone, some sixty or seventy feet high, others immense, with bright striations of color dulled by the strange flat light that threw no shadows. The wind keened across this vast amphitheater like a dirge. Snow flurries stung his eyes, and he thought it looked like the last place God made. He saw the bay's ears come up too late.

McLennon had had plenty of time to line up the shot and even in this strange, bright light, there was no way he could have blown it. Fired from no more than forty yards, the .44/40 carbine slug smashed Angel's bay down sideward in a kicking welter of dying reflexes, spilling the rider out of the saddle to hit the icy ground with enough force to knock the wind out of him. He automatically kicked his feet out of the stirrups and rolled clear of the horse. The animal was thrashing in its death throes, its bright blood staining the virgin whiteness of the snow. Angel kept rolling, and then came up on one knee, hearing the whisper of slugs as the flat hard smack of the guns opened up, the dull pock as they smashed into the snow, his eyes searching for cover, any cover. There wasn't any: they'd picked a spot where the nearest boulder was fifty yards away, where he was out in a wide open space of flat clean snow, as easy to see as a spider on a whitewashed wall. Through the keening wind, he heard the flat *blat* of a carbine, felt the slow tug of a bullet that ripped through his heavy blanket coat as if it were paper, turning him slightly offbalance for a moment. Again and again the carbines banged, and he was moving, rolling, weaving, ducking, running, covered in snow, breath already ragged as the seeking slugs whipped gouts of powder snow glinting into the air. It sifted down on him as he slid to a heaving stop, orienting himself for the last nothing-to-lose dash. He knew that it was a miracle he hadn't already been cut down, that only the strange flat light was saving him. He came up off his knees and ran now, not dodging anymore, dismissing from his mind any fear of being hit, forgetting everything except his one single, supreme effort to reach the big boulder perhaps a hundred feet away. He had no thought of anything except his intention and his destination. He ran like the wind and he was ten yards from safety when Curtis stepped out from behind the rock toward which he was running and levered the action of the Winchester, smiling a smile that would have made Satan envious.

'Hello, sucker,' he said, and pulled the trigger.

On the night of October 12, the night that Frank Angel watched the storm from his window in Buena Vista, George Willowfield broke jail. In doing so he not only killed John Henderson's deputy Steve Jackman, not only stole a wagon and team worth – according to its aggrieved owner – a good thousand dollars, but also changed the scenario that he had given Falco out of all recognition.

Willowfield was many things, not all of them either nice or acceptable in decent society, but one of the things he was not was a fool. While he had languished in jail, he had considered and reconsidered every aspect of the triple cross he had so carefully planned. The holdup of the Freedom Train had been simple and uncomplicated. The robbery of the Special carrying the ransom equally straight forward. The setting of the hound upon the hares, and the security of knowing whichever killed which, it would make not one thin dime's worth of difference to George Montefiore Willowfield.

The planned ambush of himself and his escort somewhere above Fort Morgan would not take place, even if Falco and the others made it there on schedule, for one very simple reason: Willowfield would not be going under escort back to Julesburg. To repeat: he was not a fool. He knew exactly what kind of man Chris Falco was, and had no intention of delivering himself like a lamb to Falco's slaughter. By the time Falco discovered he had been duped – if he ever discovered it – Willowfield would have recovered the ransom money and disappeared to New Orleans – perhaps even Europe. He had always wanted to visit the Uffizi in Florence. He allowed himself the faintest, the very faintest touch of regret over Buddy, who had been a most winning young man, but he shrugged it away. The world was full of winning young men like Buddy and they were all drawn ineluctably by the sweet green smell of money. He smiled fatly in the silence of his cell.

He'd been a model prisoner. Henderson and his men had thoroughly enjoyed the fat man's eye-openers about the places he had been, the *souks* of the Middle East, the Casbah in Algiers, the steamy Marseille waterfront, the jewelled waters of Positano, the gilded mansions of the rich back East – even if they weren't true, they made a damned pleasant change from talk of horses, crops, and weather. Nobody enjoyed them more than Deputy Steve Jackman, who had asked for and gotten permission to play chess with the fat man. There was no danger of Willowfield making a break: even Henderson realized the truth of that. Why, the man couldn't get four blocks before he'd fall down, winded, beached like some great soft whale. Willowfield was no damned trouble at all, not even complaining about the rotten food, and Henderson knew just how lousy it was. What he didn't know was how persuasive the fat man's honeyed tongue could be, and what he simply couldn't know was exactly how cold-blooded Willowfield actually was. One day they'd joked about the date the escort was due to arrive: October thirteenth.

'Not your lucky day, Colonel,' Henderson had said. Everyone called the fat man 'Colonel.' It seemed suitable, somehow.

'Well, sir,' Willowfield had breathed. 'There are those, you know, who would tell you that luck, or chance, or whatever you care to call it, is worth about what a cat can lick off its backside. It is the man who relies on himself, and not on luck, who makes his mark on the world. Don't you agree, sir?'

Henderson had laughingly agreed, and he was to recall that remark much later, and remember too that the fat man had not been laughing. He put it out of his mind and went about his chores. At eight, Jackman took over the night swing, and Henderson walked down Larimer Street to the Denver Queen for a couple of drinks before he turned in for the night.

Nobody ever found out where Willowfield had gotten the knife. It was surmised that he must have had it on him someplace all the time, although Marshal Henderson, whose efficiency and reputation were at stake, stoutly refused to accept that Willowfield could have concealed a knife from his search. Not that it made any damned odds at all: Steve Jackman was just as dead. From the way they found the place, they figured that what must have happened was that Jackman had set up the chessboard – the pieces were scattered all over the floor – and that somehow, incredibly, Willowfield had persuaded Steve to open up the cell door. As soon as he did, Willowfield had slid about nine inches of steel between Jackman's ribs as callously and professionally as a paid ladrone.

Old Enoch Gordon's wagon and team were hitched outside a store next to the 'Floradora' about six blocks down and two across from the jail. Enoch was inside cutting the dust, and when he came out and found his transportation missing, the manure hit the fan. Someone said later that he'd seen a hell of a fat guy climbing into the wagon. He remembered it especially because of the way the springs had squeezed down almost flat with the man's weight, and how the horses had thrown themselves against their collars to get rolling. The man said he had stood and watched as Willowfield tooled the rig north along Larimer, heading – he supposed – for the Fort Collins road, and due north toward Cheyenne. It had never occurred to him that Willowfield was not only a fugitive, but also a thief, and by the time Enoch Gordon came out of the saloon and raised a yell, Willowfield had the kind of start that no posse was going to make up. Henderson went through the motions, but his heart wasn't in it. Willowfield might have headed anywhere, north, south, east, west or any point of the compass in between. There wasn't a cat in hell's chance of catching him. The fat man was free as a bird.

TWELVE

Anyone else would have been dead.

When Angel saw Gil Curtis step out from behind the sheltering rock, the carbine leveled at his hip, he instinctively changed direction, doing the only thing he was able to do in the instant of time he had before the flame blossomed from the muzzle of the Winchester. There was precious damned hope that Curtis would miss, but that was no reason at all to stand there and let him make a killing shot. Angel went down and forward in the snow and as he did so, he corkscrewed his body to the right, kicking up a flurry of snow with his legs to try to confuse Curtis's aim.

The bullet smacked him as he rolled, dragging a shout of pain from him as it burned a wicked furrow five inches long across his bunched back muscle. Now, as Curtis levered the action of the Winchester, he had a second, not more, and in that second he had thrown the knife. A long time back, when he had first started working for the Justice Department, Angel had drawn up a set of requirements: he wanted weapons that fitted a particular specification. First, a man should be able to kill with them. Second, they should not be firearms. Third, they should be as difficult for a man looking for weapons to find as

possible, and fourth, they should not be heavy. He had
spent hours and hours with the Armorer in his workshop
below ground on the Tenth Street side of the department
building. Among the fruits of their discussions had been a
specially made pair of boots of the type called 'mule-ears'
– on account of the pull-on tabs stitched to their sides –
whose outer and inner leather was separated slightly on
the exterior side. Into the aperture the Armorer had
stitched special sheaths. Inside those sheaths nestled twin
flat-bladed Solingen steel throwing knives honed to razor
sharpness. It was one of these knives which now glinted
dully in the graying light and thudded into Curtis' body,
just below the breastbone. Curtis' eyes bulged outward.
His hands abandoned the half-cocked Winchester and
moved, hesitantly, toward the thing in his chest. His hands
plucked halfheartedly at the quivering rubber-covered
shaft of the knife, and his head sank slowly, as if the man
was afraid to confront himself with visual confirmation of
the weapon, afraid to let the brain receive the message
that the rigid sliver of steel had already sliced his heart
open.

His eyes came up to look at Frank Angel, and then a
dreadful thick gout of blood gushed from his sagging
mouth and he went down face first into the snow, as silent
as some unseen tree in some undiscovered forest. Angel
had scooped up the Winchester and was behind the rock
before Curtis had even stopped twitching. He wasted no
time on the fallen man: from the moment he had released
his hold on the knife, Angel had known that Curtis was a
dead man. Eyes narrowed, he tried now to see across the
glooming gray space to the rocks on the far side of the trail
from which the shot which had killed the bay had come.
Falco? McLennon? Which of them was over there? Were

both of them over there? And where were the horses?

He took stock of his situation. Curtis's bullet had cut across his back, and he could feel the sticky warmth of congealing blood, but there was no way he could check how bad the wound was. The fact that he could move both arms without discomfort was an indication that it wasn't serious, although that was whistling past the graveyard. He had a rifle and a sixgun, and enough ammunition. There was food in the saddlebags of his dead horse. If the weather held, he could probably last out. The sky was still clear, although it was dull now, and there was a soft gray mistiness in the lower valley. He was behind a huge rock, perhaps twenty feet high and nearly twice as many wide. It stood like a sentinel on the right hand side of the almost-invisible trail he had been following. Up the trail, to Angel's right, and perhaps three hundred yards away, another even larger one loomed. To the left lay the twin buttes guarding the entrance to the pass through which he had come. Behind him, the snow-covered open ground rose sharply to the face of a cliff striated with snow and jagged lines. In front of him was the bare expanse of snow on which the dead bay lay, its body already lightly frosted with windblown snow. Beyond it, about another fifty yards away, was a huddle of huge boulders like the one Angel was using for shelter. Two great chunks of stone were in the center, and three smaller ones were scattered nearby. One of them at least had to be there, he thought; that was where the shot that killed the horse came from. The other? Up the trail, behind the big rock?

'Falco!' he yelled. The effort of shouting sent a light-ning-flash of pain down the wound in his back. He worked his right arm. No stiffness. Yet, he reminded himself.

'Falco!' he shouted again.

121

His voice bounced around the open space, but neither sound nor movement greeted it. He looked up at the sky. The gray dullness was softening, turning pearly. Visibility was decreasing rapidly. He gauged the distances: the rocks opposite were maybe a hundred and fifty yards away. The big rock up the trail, perhaps twice that. He gave himself a moment, knowing what he had to do now.

To use the time, he slid the knife out of Curtis' body and methodically cleaned it, not thinking about what he was doing, emptying his mind of reaction or regret. His breathing rate slowed, softened, as he concentrated upon the very center of himself, the *ch'i* that Kee Lai had taught him. When he was quite ready, he stepped out into the open, crouched and wary, and moved across the whiteness toward the rocks opposite.

Buddy McLennon saw Angel come out from behind the rock on the far side of the trail and couldn't believe his eyes. Angel looked like some strange bug against the changing whitenesses, and McLennon cuddled the stock of his carbine to his cheek, taking plenty of time to pick up the target squarely in the notched backsight. Slow, he told himself, easy, watching the little black bug that was Angel. Squeeze, *squeeze*. The Winchester bucked and the moaning wind whipped away the smoke in a flurry of fine snow. The little black bug was still moving, coming nearer. How the hell could he have missed? McLennon cursed. He lined up the carbine again, wondering why Falco didn't take a poke at Angel from where he was up the trail, and pulled off another shot at the weaving, dodging figure. Again he missed, and he fired twice more in rapid succession as the icy fingers of panic touched his heart. Was the man unkillable? The flurry of shots had told the dodging Angel what he wanted to know. The one behind the rock was McLennon. Falco would have known after the first shot that the light, which was deteriorating at a very rapid rate, was making him miss. The fact that Falco had not pitched in with a try for the target Angel had made of himself showed that Falco knew only too well that this strange light would foreshorten distance to such an extent that accurate long-range shooting would be difficult for a cool-headed expert, and nearly hopeless for anyone who panicked as easily as the kid. Short range, however, was something else again. He kept moving, and prayed that McLennon didn't know about that either.

He didn't.

He just saw Frank Angel coming on through the deep snow and threw another shot at him. When that didn't have any effect, Buddy McLennon jumped down off his rock and, levering the action of the carbine, stumbled forward through the snow toward Angel, shouting curses as he came.

Sitting duck, Angel thought without pity.

He knelt down in the snow and put three bullets through Buddy McLennon at sixty-five yards. There wasn't a hand span between them and they tore the life out of the kid in a bursting bloody spray that turned the snow behind his whacked-down body pink within a radius of four feet. Angel wasted no time on the fallen McLennon, but ran as fast as he could through the drag of the snow, heading for the rocks from which the kid had emerged.

No horses. That meant Falco had the horses. It also meant that Angel was in deep trouble. Almost as if Falco had read his mind, Angel heard the soft, snow-muffled thump of hoofs moving on the soft snow and he caught movement up the trail. Falco was moving out, heading up the long valley of the pass toward the no longer visible slopes. They were now hidden behind the misting grayness that had come up from the lower valleys. The sky had turned the color of lead left outdoors, and the wind was making a sound not far from the whine of anguish. Snow, which had moments before touched his face like feathers, now had a cutting edge that whipped red rawness across Angel's cheekbones. Beneath the heavy blanket coat he felt the soft pull of the drying blood sticking to his shirt. He stood by the huge rocks, the useless carbine in his hanging hand, eyes bleak and empty.

And then the blizzard was upon him.

One minute he was out in the open, the air chilling, the light leaden, the wind sharpening. The next minute there was a roar as if some mighty machine had started turning and the wind came up out of the valley like the exhalation of a dying giant, whipping the snow off the sharp crests of the drifts in a horizontal hail that battered and snatched, slashed and rocked him, taking his breath away with its sudden ferocity. Floundering, blinded, his sense of direction gone completely in the few seconds that it had taken for the blizzard to spring up, and fighting down the chill of panic, Angel cursed himself, cursed his stupidity in not reading the signs fast enough. The gray mist that had been creeping up the slopes like soapy water, the strange light, all had been warnings. He should have read them as clearly as those first dancing flurries of snow, the icy edge of the wind. Now its howling gale force cut through his layered clothing as if it were tissue paper. The long wound on his back ached raw as the icy fingers of the blizzard found it; his bloodstained coat was already frozen stiff. His leg went down to the crotch in deep snow and he could no longer even see the faint traces of the trail he had been standing on.

He dragged himself up out of the clutching snow, fighting off the soft insistent chill of it, laboring up an incline in what he hoped was the direction that Falco had taken. His mouth sagged open and the wind tore his breath out of it as it drove an incessant hail of minuscule ice splinters against his skin, scouring his face to raw pink and then flat white in minutes. It pushed and bullied his staggering body offbalance, and if he had not strapped down the brim of his Stetson with his neckerchief to protect his ears, and a wool scarf around his face, he would have been frostbitten in no time. The wind rattled and flurried and harassed him. The brim of his Stetson beat in a frenzied staccato against his cheeks, making red marks.

He labored on.

A hundred yards, perhaps. More? He was exhausted when the wind stopped as abruptly as it had begun and he saw that, miraculously, he was close to the big rock behind which Falco had hidden. He silently thanked whatever gods were guiding his footsteps in the right directions, and staggered through the silent snow past the big rock and up toward the long crest that sloped away beyond it. He did not bother to look for tracks: the snow and wind would have scoured them away almost as soon as they were made. He broke into a lumbering run, his breath ragged. Although he was already worn down, he knew he had to cover as much ground as he could before the blizzard broke loose again. This was nothing but a momentary respite. He found he was still clutching the Winchester and he threw it away without a second's hesitation. It landed barrel-down in the snow like a spear, remaining upright, stuck in the empty whiteness as if it were marking a grave.

Angel had covered about a quarter of a mile – during

which time he remembered he had not taken any food from the saddlebags on the dead horse – when the wind opened up again. There was nothing he could do but turn his back to it like any other animal, hunching down in misery away from the slashing, seeking, incessant attack of the blizzard, seeing nothing but empty whirling whiteness, hearing nothing but the roaring howl of the wind and the soft sibilant sound of the snow sliding across the icy surface. He stood stoically through endless minutes of mind-emptied waitfulness, not thinking, not hoping, not doing anything until, as if gathering its strength for a final assault, the wind eased, sagged, dropped away. A fitful, watery patch of sunlit blue sky showed for an instant through swirling cloud. By the time it had opened up slightly, Angel was already moving up the hill. He went at it with the desperate strength of a man without much in reserve. The slope faced north and the snow was deep and crisp. It covered the rocks and gullies with a deceptive layer of whipped-cream softness. If Angel put too much weight on his feet, he sank into it to the hip. He had to move fast, yet lightly on his feet, keeping his balance against the playful bluster of the wind. The slope seemed endless, endless. His breath came shallower now in the thin mountain air and his lips were as dry as if he were in some waterless desert. It wasn't a long slope, perhaps not more than two hundred and fifty yards. He could see the crest, soft and rounded against the sky ahead. It wasn't physically far away but it took him the best part of thirty minutes to get two-thirds of the way up it and by the time he got there he was almost weeping with fatigue. He looked back downhill at the painfully traced line of boot-holes he had left. They seemed so pathetically few that it was almost impossible to believe they had taken so much out of him. He put his head down and went on. To keep his feet moving he chanted an old work song under his breath. There was nobody to witness his heroism, nobody to cheer. And when he got to the top and saw that beyond this slope lay another, identical one, it almost broke his heart.

He stood on the crest, knee-deep in the sifting snow, his shoulders laboring like some cruelly treated animal. He shook his head. He could not go any further, nor could he retrace his steps. He wanted to sit down, to rest. The wound in his back was on fire, and one small part of his brain was trying to persuade him that it didn't really matter, anyway, that it wasn't worth the effort, that there was no place to hide, no place to find shelter. Beyond the next slope would be another and beyond that another. In this gleaming hostile wilderness, what difference did it make which pile of snow you died in?

He made himself get up and walk.

Right. Left. Right foot. Left foot. Keep going, he told himself, just a bit further. Right foot. Left foot. Just a bit further. Then he saw the deep wide trenches in the snow made by the horses and he felt a gush of relief. Not only was he on the right track, but Falco was in as much trouble as he was himself. The horses looked as if they were out of hand, if the tracks were anything to go by. Bucking snow was an art natural only to the native-born mustang. Domesticated animals seldom acquired the art, and were inclined always to lunge at the snow rather than work their way through it. Even the wiry cayuse would sometimes give out after working its way through snow up to its belly for a few hours. Falco's horses wouldn't last another hour if the tracks on the snow were anything to go by. Angel grinned grimly beneath the wool scarf and plodded on, moving easier now in the flattened snow of the horses' passage. The edge of the wind whipped at the skin of his face that was exposed and he prayed for the blizzard to hold off. He got halfway up the long empty slope. It seemed as if he had been walking forever. He had no thought except the thought of putting one foot in front of the other foot, no sense of time, nothing except the single-minded aim to survive.

When he got to the crest of the long second slope he saw the cabin. It lay about a quarter of a mile away, on the flank of another long slope that stretched away downward from where Angel now stood. Falco's tracks led directly toward it and he nodded as he saw them. The powder snow whipped off the edge of the crest in a knife-edge line that whitened the creases in the icy mush that had formed on his clothing, and Angel drove his wilting body down the slope, below the lee of the crest where he could shelter for a moment from the biting, growing rush of the wind, drawing upon his last reservoirs of strength. I can make it, he told himself. I can make it now. The wind moaned and then screamed and then opened its throat with a banshee wail as it clamped down the blizzard upon the mountains with an awful, intense finality. It blew Angel across the empty face of the slope as if he were a child's rag doll, bowling him over face down. He straggled, spitting and kicking, out of the drift of snow into which he had been hurled, trying desperately to orient himself in the howling whiteness, not knowing that he was screaming at the wind as if it were some live thing attacking him.

'Damn you!' he shouted. 'Damn you, damn you, goddamn you!'

He found that he was on his knees in the snow, and he had lost his gloves someplace. His hands looked dirty white against the purer whiteness of the snow. The roaring wind surrounded him, swallowed him. He was blinded, engulfed in the whirling surge of the powder snow laced with ice that was torn from the face of the mountain. Somehow he got to his feet and moved. Forward? He felt for the rise of the slope, but he could sense nothing. His feet were like wooden blocks, his face stiff and numb, his hands without feeling. He walked straight into a flat upright rock, caroming off it before he had even seen it properly, gashing his cheekbone against the jagged stone. Sobbing with relief, he worked his way around behind the big rock, into the sheltering lee where he was shielded from the searching wind. Up ahead of him he sensed, rather than truly saw, the hulking dark bulk of the cabin. He didn't want to move, didn't want to have to walk that far again or go out into the murderous hail of snow and ice but he knew he must. If he stayed here now he would die.

The wind was a familiar enemy now, and seconds after he started moving in it he felt as if he had never stopped. Numb, dumb, weightless, without form, he was an animal hunting a place to cower away from the awesome fury of nature. He had no ambition now except to survive. That alone would be enough.

He remembered nothing more until he walked into the pile of logs behind the cabin. His numb body registered the impact, and he fell to his knees in the soft snow, groping his way around the log pile until he was in the space between it and the cabin. It was dark and warm, compared to the raging cold on the other side. He squirmed around, barking his knuckles on the frozen logs of the cabin wall. It didn't matter if he made a noise. In this wind nobody would hear a sound. He sat up, chafing his hands, rubbing them hard against each other. Then he rubbed snow on his half-frozen face, punishing the skin. Slowly, very slowly, he felt the blood tingling into the deadened veins, felt the warm pulse of life spread from his belly, felt himself coming back. He just sat there, ice melting into water that mixed with the tears of fatigue from his eyes, dripping from his chin. He looked at his hands. They felt like two bunches of bananas, and something like a grin twisted his frozen features.

He was in great shape for a fight, he thought.

THIRTEEN

As suddenly as it had started, the blizzard stopped. Almost immediately, the sky began to clear, and the wind dropped away. In half an hour the sky was an astonishingly bright cerulean blue, the way it is only in the high mountains. The enormous presence of the serried peaks themselves now became visible. They reared up over the pass, dazzling the eye in the sunlight with their white covering of fresh snow. Now small animals moved tentatively in the sparse trees, and black birds sought food again. Their presence was strangely reassuring. The horses shifted restlessly in the lean-to behind the cabin, stamping and snorting, hoping for something to eat.

Angel had moved from behind the woodpile as soon as he was able and scuttled across to the lean-to which housed the horses. From it, he could see Falco moving about in the lighted cabin, but he stayed in the lean-to until the warmth of the animals revived him. In one of the saddlebags, he found some small strips of jerky and he had chewed it with famished enjoyment, milking the strength from the dried meat and feeling it warm him. It was still sparklingly, bitingly cold, too cold for him to take off his clothes and clean up his wounded back. It was stiff with clotted blood now, and most of his left shoulder felt numb to the touch, as though the skin had died. He could still move his arm, but it didn't feel right.

The dark brown smell of coffee touched his nostrils and his mouth was instantly full of saliva. He remembered Pat O'Connor sitting in the train, saying, 'I could kill for coffee!'

He edged to the front of the lean-to and saw smoke coming from the tin chimney atop the cabin. Moving on silent feet, he skirted the cabin and eased up on to the wooden porch at the front. The thick snow muffled the slight scrape of his boots. He put his weight on the door and went in all at once with the sixgun in his hand, and a grin like a killing wolf on his face.

He caught Falco cold.

Falco was just lifting a blackened coffee pot off the top of a potbellied stove that stood at the end of the room opposite the door. As the door opened, Falco whirled around, the brown coffee making a long, steaming arc from the lip of the pot, splattering on the floor. His sixgun was in the holster on the belt hanging on a peg to Angel's right, next to his coat. His carbine was propped up against the same wall. Between them and him was the oilcloth-covered table. Angel saw him check off all the possibilities and discard them in the space of two deep breaths, and then Falco's shoulders dropped just that inch.

Stone cold, the movement said, and Angel nodded.

'That's it, Falco,' he said. 'While you're up, pour me a cup.'

Falco looked at Angel and the thinnest hint of a smile touched his mouth.

'You're hard to kill, mister,' he said. 'You ought to be dead.'

'I damned nearly am,' Angel told him. 'Sit down.'

He gestured to a chair on the far side of the table from the wall on which Falco's coat and guns were hanging. Then he went around to the opposite side of the table and pulled out the chair from beneath it. The stove was on his right, and it was glowing with heat. The wood inside spat and crackled. He watched Falco as the gray-haired man poured another tin mug full of coffee and pushed it across to him. Not until Falco sat down and picked up his own coffee cup did Angel drink any of his own. It tasted like the nectar of the gods.

'You make good coffee,' he said. 'You married?'

'What?' Falco said.

'Nothing,' Angel said. 'What's in the pot there?'

There was a heavy iron pot standing on the flat top of the stove. It gave off a slight bubbling sound.

'Just beans,' Falco said. 'All there was.'

'I hope you got enough for four,' Angel told him. Falco frowned.

'You got more people with you?'

'Nope,' Angel replied. 'I plan to eat enough for three.'

Falco shrugged. Angel was cocky enough now, but that was now. There had to be a way to copper the bet, and he started figuring, figuring, as he sipped his coffee. Angel had been out in that blizzard, right? No food, nothing to drink. He'd be worn down by just staying alive. He'd need rest. The warm cabin, plenty of hot food would make him drowsy. Sooner or later he'd have to sleep. And that would be that. It was just a question of keeping cool, Falco thought. He made his tensed muscles relax.

'You don't look too good, Angel,' he said.

Angel grinned his wolf grin. 'I've been healthier,' he admitted.

'You hurt?'

133

'I don't know,' Angel admitted. 'Your boy Curtis put some kind of a hole in me, but it's in my back, and I can't see it.'

'Turn around,' Falco suggested with a cold grin. 'I'll take a look at it.'

'Oh, sure,' Angel said.

'Just trying to help.'

'I'll bet.'

There was a silence.

'What makes you try so hard, Angel?' Falco asked, finally. 'Plenty of others would have just given up, backed off, gone home.'

'You really want to know?'

'Yeah,' Falco said. 'Tell me, I really want to know.'

'It's simple enough,' Angel said. 'If you were ordinary, everyday, common-garden variety killers, I might have let you run, and just put out a handbill on you. But you made it personal. You tried to kill me. And more than that: you killed a friend of mine.'

'On the Special, you mean?'

'On the Special,' Angel said. 'His name was Bob Little. He was a good man, Falco. He had a nice wife and a little kid named Joey and someone has to go and tell them that he isn't coming home anymore.'

'You, Angel?'

'Me,' Angel said grimly. 'I'll do it. But when I do it, I want at least to be able to tell Barbara Little that the men who killed her husband have been taken care of.'

His last three words hung in the air, and Falco swallowed noisily.

'What you planning to do with me, Angel?' he asked. 'Kill me cold?'

'Oh, no,' Angel said. 'No, I'm taking you in, Falco.

They're going to hang you. Higher than a kite.'

He said it with such implacability that for a moment, Falco saw a mental picture of himself with the hood over his head, standing on a wooden scaffold in some rain-gray prison yard. Then his self-confidence surged back. What was he afraid of? Here was Angel exhausted, wounded, played out. He could take him when ready. Easy as pie.

'Easier said than done, Angel,' he said. 'I won't hang so easy. You may have just gotten yourself a tiger by the tail.'

He laughed harshly at his own humor, but Angel's contemptuous stare stilled the sound.

'You're no tiger, Falco,' Angel said. 'A pussycat, maybe.'

A frown darkened Falco's face.

'What's that supposed to mean?' he glowered.

'Why, it means you've been flim-flammed, Falco,' Angel said, mirthlessly. 'You mean you didn't know it?'

'Flim-flammed?' Falco burst out. 'How do you mean, flim-flammed?'

Angel shook his head, his expression saying that he didn't know there were still people on the earth this dumb.

'Willowfield,' he explained patiently. 'He's left you holding the bag. Haven't you cottoned on yet?'

Falco shook his head. He wasn't falling for this. No way. Angel was trying to push him offbalance, getting him to commit something that he didn't yet recognize. Well, he wasn't having any. None of your psychology games today, Angel. No getting me on edge, no pushing me offbalance. I know what I've got to do. Kill you, get the hell out of here. Kill the fat man, grab the loot, and take off. Life is that simple and nothing you can say will complicate it more.

'Falco,' Angel was saying. 'There's one thing I don't

135

know, and need to know. Which of you stole the Declaration of Independence?'

Despite the vows he'd just made to himself, Falco's mouth fell agape at Angel's unexpected words, and Frank Angel nodded as though that in itself was all the answer he had expected.

'Uh huh,' he said. 'It figured.'

'What is this?' bleated Falco. 'You telling me someone stole the—'

'Shut up,' Angel told him. 'And listen. I'll tell you what happened. You tell me afterward where I got it wrong – if anywhere. Listen: Willowfield had someone on his payroll at the marshal's office in Denver, right?'

'Right,' Falco agreed, warily. No harm in Angel knowing that now. 'Some jerk deputy. Steve Jackman, his name was.'

'Who passed the word along to one of you in Denver about the date of the escort's arrival to take Willowfield back east. Who was it, Curtis?'

'McLennon,' Falco said.

'McLennon,' Angel nodded. 'So McLennon brought the word down to Canon City that I was on the way, and that Willowfield would leave Denver under escort on October thirteenth. All you had to do was waste me, circle back to Denver, light out after the escort, wipe them out and spring Willowfield. If I was doing that, I'd probably do it around Two Mile Creek. How about it?'

He didn't need an answer; the look on Falco's face told him he was right on the button, and he pressed relentlessly on.

'What then? Head for the cache, split the loot, and punch a hole in the breeze, I'd say. Nice and neat and tight. Except for one thing, Falco, except for one thing.'

'What?' Falco said, trying for a jeer. 'What one thing, smartass?'

'Willowfield,' Angel explained. 'He read you like a book, Falco. Anybody could. I can. You never had any intention of springing the fat man, did you? You were going to ice him and the escort at the same time, and if any of your sidekicks had given you a hard time, you'd probably have blown them up as well.'

'No,' Falco said, as if hypnotized by Angel's voice. 'No need of that. The boys knew what I was going to do. Only we didn't figure on you—'

'Being so hard to kill?' Angel grinned, without humor. 'Boy, Falco, you really are a pussycat. I wouldn't put you in charge of an empty corral. Well,' he sighed theatrically. 'You'll take the rap for the whole show. And not a dime to show for it.'

'Yeah?' said Falco. He was really having to reach for defiance now, and his unease was showing quite plainly. 'How do you figure that?'

Angel shook his head wearily, the movement of a man exasperated with someone so dull that he cannot understand why a wheel rolls. 'Willowfield had a man in the marshal's office, right?' he asked.

'Right.'

'Today is October 13,' Angel reminded him.

'So.'

'So do you think the fat man is going to be sitting waiting for that escort to come and take him back to Leavenworth to hang?'

Now Falco got it and his eyes turned sick. Although Angel was guessing the worst way, it got right to the gray-haired man. On his face was the expression a man might wear as he watched his home and everything he possessed being washed away by a flood he was powerless to control.

'That bastard,' he whispered. 'That fat old bastard!'

His mind was awhirl with anger and frustration. If what Angel said was true – and it probably was, it had the right ring about it – then Willowfield had set him up like a patsy. All that work, all that hard graft for nothing. That fat old obscenity would have the lot. He had used them all as casually and contemptuously as a whiskey drummer using hotel notepaper. Anger boiled up in him. He knew now he couldn't wait. Hours, even minutes had become vital. There were three horses in the lean-to outside. If he killed two of them, he could be in Denver on the third by late evening. A train to Cheyenne, another east to Julesburg. If Willowfield had beaten him to the cache, Willowfield could only go one way – east. He could not travel unnoticed, not Willowfield, so he would be easy to find and a pleasure to kill. If the fat man hadn't reached the cache, then Falco would wait until he came and kill him then.

But first he had to kill Angel.

'Listen,' he said, not looking at his captor lest his decision reveal itself on his face or in his eyes. 'Why would he have taken that Declaration of Independence. What the hell use would that be?'

'Probably for the reason he gave when he told me you'd stolen it,' Angel said, reflectively. 'An ace in the hole. A way to buy time, maybe, or make a deal with whoever came after him.'

'And could he?'

'Make a deal? No way.'

'What about me?'

'No deals for you, either, Falco. You go into Fairplay with me. You can sweat it out in the jail while I go after Willowfield. He'll be heading up for where you wrecked the Special. I guess you hid the money somewhere up near there.'

There was no harm in telling him, Falco thought. He'd be dead in a few minutes, anyway. Give him something to lull him a little, why not? 'On the treeline,' he said. 'About a mile west of the gully, just above the trail. There's a blaze on the tree it's buried under. A letter "W".'

He made a show of sniffing, and then lifted his chin, pointing at the iron pot on top of the pot-bellied stove. 'Them beans need eating,' he said. 'Before they burn.'

'Dish them up,' Angel said. 'We can get finished and ride on into Fairplay while there's still plenty of light. And Falco . . .' He made a small gesture with the sixgun, more to draw attention to it than anything else. 'Don't you go and do anything that might prove fatal, now.'

Falco nodded, and got up out of the chair slowly, keeping his hands where Angel could see them as he crossed the room toward the stove.

Angel pulled his chair closer to the table, and switched the sixgun from his left hand to his right, and, as he did, Falco, who had lifted the heavy cast-iron pot from the top of the stove with his left hand, swung it in a tight wicked arc from the stove around toward Angel's head. Angel did the only thing he possibly could. He went backward in his chair, spilling over on to the ground as the iron pot whammed through the space where his head had been. Beans spattered all over the wall and the table in a steaming sticky mess as Angel hit the floor with the gun cocked and up. Although he'd been ready to crease Falco, the impact of his wounded shoulder on the bare boards drove a shuddering smash of pain through his entire left side, and the gun dropped unfired from his nerveless fingers. In that same second Falco kicked the table aside and dived with his hands outstretched for Angel's throat.

Angel eeled desperately to one side as Falco's thrusting fingers pawed his neck. Then Falco's knees, with all his weight on them, slammed into Angel's belly, doubling him up retching, the wind whacked out of him. Falco scrambled to his feet and kicked the writhing man hard in the left side and drew his foot back for another kick. Angel saw it coming and rolled first to the right and then the left, avoiding Falco's stomping boots. The soft warmth of fresh-flowing blood spread beneath his clothes. His eyes were still not properly focused but he came up on to his knees and saw that Falco was diving for the nickel-plated Colt hanging holstered on the wall peg, snatching it out and whirling, his eyes as malevolent as those of a stoat loose in a rabbithole. He was earing back the hammer and his mouth was twisted with the lust to kill. Angel's knife was already in flight.

It flicked across the space between the two men just as Falco completed his turn. It sheared through the *flexor capri radialis* of his right arm as if that solid forearm muscle were butter, and pinned it to the log wall like some bizarre trophy. Falco screamed with undiluted pain, his sixgun dropping from a hand whose controlling tendons no longer worked. His eyes bugged as he looked at the pinned arm and then his head turned to face Angel, but in that moment Angel had moved across the room at Falco, his right arm drawn back, with the edge of his hand held level like a machete. He smashed it horizontally against Falco's forehead, and the gray-winged head went back against the log wall with a sound like someone hitting a fence post with a wooden mallet. Falco's eyes rolled up in his head and his knees wilted.

As the man started to fall, Angel plucked the knife clear

of the wall and Falco slid off the blade and down to the blood-spattered floor. His right arm lay askew, like a broken wing.

Angel knelt quickly and checked Falco's pulse: the throb of the carotid artery was strong. He rose to his full height, shaking his head.

'This "capture not kill" game'll be the death of me yet,' he sighed, as he scouted around for material to use for bandaging Falco's arm. When he had done this, he tore up a blanket from the bunk in the corner of the room and used it to bind Falco's arm to his body, and then his good arm to the ruined one. Using the deadly 'Chink's knot' which ensures strangulation if the one so bound struggles against them, he tied Falco's feet to his arms to his neck.

'So,' he said, at last.

He put some water on to boil and then went across to where the iron pot that had contained the beans lay on its side. There was still enough in it for one man. He looked around at the rest, splattered on the table and the walls and the floor, and grinned as he spooned what was left on to a plate. After he had eaten, he would clean up his own wound as best he could, and then head for Fairplay with Falco. He didn't think the man would give him any more trouble. Even if he tried, it would be easy enough to handle if Falco gave off as many signals as he had before he tried the one with the bean pot. Falco could go in the slammer at Fairplay until someone could come out and bring him to Leavenworth to be hung. He settled down to eat.

'My compliments to the chef,' he said to the unconscious Falco.

FOURTEEN

It had all been so childishly easy.

George Willowfield looked out of the window of the train and smiled at the featureless prairie rushing past. Beautiful, he thought. He turned his attention to the plush interior of the Pullman car in which he was riding, thinking what a fine railroad the Union Pacific was, how comfortable, and – so important – how reliable. These Pullman sleeping cars were said to cost $20,000 apiece, and it didn't surprise him in the least. The fittings and hoods and lamps and rails all looked to be silver-plated, and the upholsteries and carpets were all first class. The very paneling looked to be walnut, b'God. Behind this carriage rolled an equally luxurious restaurant car in which, earlier, Willowfield had eaten a most ample and satisfying meal. Yes, this was the way to travel: first class all the way. He knew, as anyone who had ever traveled by rail knew, that the emigrant coaches would be full of noisy, dirty travelers with even noisier and dirtier brats whom they fed at all hours of the day or night with no regard to common decency, while great stinking Indians smoked foul tobacco or drank rum until they passed out.

No, he thought, never again. From here on, first class all the way for you, my dear George. He sighed with pleasure, his fingers softly stroking the velvet carpetbag on his lap, as if it were a living thing. He wondered what that attractive young man he'd taken a smile with in the depot at Ogallala would have thought had he known what was in the carpetbag, then chided himself upon such thoughts. There would be time enough for that when he reached his destination. He smiled again, the smile of the fox who knows the hounds will never catch him.

The conductor came through the car, calling, 'Next stop Cheyenne. Cheyenne in twenty-eight minutes!'

Willowfield nodded. The Union Pacific Railroad was as reliable as ever. He looked out of the window at the mountains like clouds on the long horizon, remembering.

He had driven the stolen wagon to the junction of the trail south of old Fort Collins, then veered east to follow the road that led down alongside a rushing torrent whose name he did not know. At the point where it joined the north fork of the Platte, he forded the bigger river and worked his way northeasterly, using a compass he had bought in a ship's chandler in St. Joseph, Missouri, long before all of this had started, even when he did not know the outcome for sure. Planning, he thought, smiling. Everything is planning, as any good cook will tell you. He rode well clear of settlements, stopping only at one gritty, flea-bitten wayside cluster of shacks to buy a canvas sack from a general store that looked as if it had just survived an earthquake.

By the late afternoon of the following day he was digging up the buried money in its oilskin packs, and then to Julesburg in time to buy a ticket for the east-bound train.

He had passed the place where the train carrying the money had been wrecked, and heard the sound of steam engines and hammers, of men working down in the gully and he smiled. It might have been a million years ago. He wondered briefly who had killed whom, and whether Falco or any of them were left alive. It mattered not a damn. They would never find him, for he had one trick left in his bag, and he set it in motion at Julesburg.

It was a risk, he knew, but a calculated one. The U.S. marshal at Denver might have telegraphed the fact of his surprise escape to his colleagues in other states, even to the police in the big cities, certainly to the Justice Department in Washington. It was highly unlikely that anything had sifted down to the level of a station manager at a godforsaken hole like Julesburg, which was hardly more than a clutter of houses. Hyar, they said, was the California Crossing of the South Platte; over thar, the old Pony Express station house with its outbuildings and stables and blacksmith shop made of cedar logs; just a-down yonder Jack Slade killed Jules Beni. They seemed proud of the place, and Willowfield let them see the contempt of a gentleman for it, so that they would remember him. His insistence on clean crockery and cutlery when he drank a cup of the muddy coffee they served in the refreshment room, and his lordly announcement of his name when he bought his ticket, all would be remembered when questions were asked later – as he was sure they would. The train came – on time, he recalled with pleasure – and he stepped aboard, tipping the porter, who carried his case into the carriage, a dollar to prompt his memory when the time for remembering came. He tipped the man again when he alighted from the train in Council Bluffs, making no secret of the fact that his destination was New York. The porter wished him a safe journey, as did the engineer Willowfield congratulated on a punctual arrival.

The fat man then left the station and hurried in a horse cab to the largest men's clothing emporium in the town, James & Laurence, on the corner of Front and River Streets, where he purchased a suitcase, large enough for several suits of clothing, and then outfitted himself in the manner of a man setting out on a long journey. Which, he reminded himself with a smile, he undoubtedly was.

His old clothes, while still serviceable, he no longer required, and he dropped them into a dustbin near the railroad station, knowing that some bum would hustle them off the moment night fell. Entering the same terminal he had quit not two hours before, Willowfield bought himself a first class ticket for San Francisco, and within another hour was thundering back along the route he had so recently traversed.

On his lap lay the carpetbag with the better part of a quarter of a million in it – his wardrobe had scarcely dented the pile. On the rack overhead was his traveling case. In the baggage car was his big case containing his clothes. And nestling in his inside pocket, in an oilskin wrapper, was the crackling parchment that half the law officers in the United States were looking for. He allowed himself another smile.

Well, the United States should have its Declaration of Independence back, in good time. He had not yet decided how much they should pay for it, nor exactly how he would handle the ploy. That could all wait until he reached journey's end. He recited the route ahead with loving relish: Cheyenne, Laramie, Rock Springs, Salt Lake City, Elko, Winnemucca, Reno, Sacramento, and finally, the lovely city on the bay: San Francisco.

The train was slowing on the descent into Cheyenne and he debated whether to get out and stretch his legs for five minutes, then decided against it. He leaned his head back against the plush velvet cushions of his seat, stretched his legs, and sighed, a smile of contented amusement on his face.

Catch me if you can, he thought.

'You'll live,' Doctor Hussey said.

He watched impassively as Frank Angel put back on his clothes. He had stitched up the long, raw wound, bound it as tightly as good sense dictated, and there wasn't much else he could do that nature couldn't do as well, if not better. He had tried half a dozen times to dissuade his patient from making the long ride he planned through the mountains, but to all his advice Angel had remained quite immune.

'It's got to be done,' was all he would say.

He had brought Falco down from the cabin in the mountains and reached Fairplay as night was falling. A cold wind had been sweeping down from the snowy crests to the west, but the weather was staying clear and they were able to make decent time. Angel had lodged Falco with the sheriff of Park County, whose office was in the two-story red sandstone courthouse in the center of town. Falco had been silent throughout the whole journey, nursing his ruined arm like an Indian squaw keening over her fallen brave. His eyes had no life in them at all. Angel had taken one look at the man and known he was finished. It wouldn't make any difference what happened to Falco from here on in: something inside him had broken, snapped, given way.

The doctor came to do what he could for the prisoner's arm and when he was through, Angel walked back with him to his house, a white frame shack next door to the

Presbyterian church. On the way he told Hussey that he had to make Denver by the following afternoon, nightfall at the latest.

'You'll need damned good animals,' Hussey said. 'That's a hard run.'

'I know it,' Angel replied. 'The sheriff's lining them up for me, right now.'

While he was examining the wound on Angel's back, the doctor asked a question, and Angel slid the throwing knife out of his boot.

'I used this,' he said.

Hussey tested the edge of the blade with a tentative thumb.

'I thought it must be something out of the ordinary,' he said. 'The way the muscles were sheared through.'

'I didn't have a hell of a lot of choice, Doc,' Angel said, sensing the implied censure. 'He had a cocked sixgun in his hand.'

Hussey shook his head.

'It's none of my damned business, I know,' he said gruffly. 'I just hate waste, and when I see a man with a right arm that's going to be about as much use to him from here on in as a piece of string, I. . . .'

'Don't you worry none,' Angel had assured him harshly. 'Falco's not going to live long enough to notice.'

His cold pronouncement had startled Dick Hussey, who was still young enough and idealistic enough to believe that there was innate good in even the worst of men. As a doctor, in a town as tough as Fairplay could be, he'd seen his share of mayhem and its results. He still didn't believe in the theory of a man all bad, nor was he ready for anyone who seemed to be as callous about maiming another human being as Frank Angel was, and he said so.

'It's not callousness, doc,' Angel said. 'My business is survival. I'm no damned use to the Department dead.'

'The Department,' Hussey nodded, saying it the way you'd say the name of a partner who cheated you. 'It must be quite an organization.'

'Doc,' Angel told him with a frosty smile, 'it is.'

He left then to walk down the street to the Hand Hotel, where Sheriff Graham was waiting for him. He had four horses saddled and ready, the best, he said, he could find in town.

'You won't get far at night,' he warned. 'That's a poor road up toward Silverheels.'

'Every mile gets me nearer Denver, Sheriff,' Angel said. 'And that's what I'm after.'

'You must want this Willowfield feller powerful bad,' Graham said. 'What's he done?'

'Well for one thing,' Angel said, swinging up into the saddle, 'He's lived too long.' Then he kicked the horses into a run and headed up the hill.

'All aboard!'

Willowfield heard the shouts up at the far end of the train, then the thundering shudder of the drive wheels making their first grinding turns for grip on the shining tracks. The engine exhaled deeply as she moved the train slowly out of the Cheyenne depot, and the engineer gave the town a farewell blast with his whistle as she shun-nashunnashunn'ed westward. People were resuming the seats they had vacated during the ten-minute stop and Willowfield turned his head away, watching through the window as the dun land sped past beneath the clacketing wheels of the train.

Laramie, he recited to himself: Rock Springs, Salt Lake

City, Elko, Reno, Sacramento. And San Francisco. He leaned back in the soft seat and closed his eyes. In his mind he saw himself in a darkened, paneled room. A log fire was burning, and crystal glasses caught the flickers of the flames and turned them to diamonds. He was wearing a velvet jacket with piped lapels and cuffs, soft lambswool lined slippers, thin silk pantaloons of almost oriental design. There was incense in the air, a faint perfume. Or was it the boy? Moving across the room toward him was a fair-haired youth, twenty perhaps, adoration in his eyes, submission in his posture. His voice would be fluting, breathy. Then he would. . . .

'Colonel?'

He opened his eyes and Frank Angel was sitting opposite him. Willowfield's eyes widened and he came upright in the seat, head turning this way and that. The conductor was standing at Angel's right elbow, and now the fat man noticed that the train was slowing down.

'Ah,' he said, nodding his great head. 'Ah, yes. Mister Angel. We meet again, sir.'

'Indeed we do,' Frank Angel said. 'Indeed we do. Here, let me take that bag. I'm sure you must be tired of carrying it.'

The fat man smiled as Angel lifted the carpetbag off his knees and handed it to the conductor. His eyes followed the bag, which contained all his dreams, as if attached to it with string.

'Well, sir,' he said, at last, bringing his eyes back to stare at Angel. 'You seem to have outwitted me.'

'It would look like that,' Angel said. 'We'll be back in Cheyenne in about ten minutes. There's a military escort waiting for you.'

'You are efficient, sir,' Willowfield sighed. 'I always

suspected it. Am I to assume from your presence here that Falco and the others are dead?'

'No,' Angel said. 'Falco's not dead. Nor Kuden. The others are, though.'

'Pity,' Willowfield said, and Angel did not know whether he meant that it was a pity the others were dead or that it was a pity Falco and Kuden were still alive.

Willowfield gave a long, deep sigh.

'Tell me, Mr Angel,' he said. 'Tell me, please. How did you find me? How did you do it?'

'It was easy,' Angel said, stepping hard on the fat man's ego. 'You made it easy.'

'No, sir,' Willowfield gusted, temper mottling his face. 'No, I did not. I took every precaution. Every precaution.'

'You sure did,' Angel replied. 'You laid a trail a ten-year-old kid could have followed, Willowfield. And that was your mistake.'

'Mistake, sir? How was it a mistake?'

'Because I knew you were a thief and I knew you were a killer and I knew you were a man who'd have double-crossed his mother for the price of a cigar, Willowfield, but I also knew something else: you were not a fool. So if you were laying a trail for me, then you had a trick up your sleeve. I just didn't know what it was, and I had damned little time to find out.'

He remembered how it had been, coming through the mountains, finally seeing the smoky haze above Denver on the plain below, every muscle in his body aching from the pounding ride, and two of the horses dead of exhaustion on the trail in back of him. All the way to Denver, whenever he could isolate his mind from the job of guiding his mount, he had tried to read the mind of his quarry: *When the fox runs, he will always lead away from his den.*

When he piled into the marshal's office, Henderson had confirmed everything that Angel had suspected and guessed about the fat man. They went over to the express office, and once more commandeered the telegraph.

Messages chattered across the wires between Washington and Denver well into the night, as Frank Angel gave full reports of his own activities, and information was fed back to him of departmental investigations into Willowfield's movements.

'He was seen boarding a train in Julesburg,' Angel told Henderson, 'and the porter recalls him leaving it at Council Bluffs. Our men found a hobo wearing a coat with Willowfield's name stitched into it, which suggested he'd either been killed, or fitted himself out with new clothes. The hobo was clean, no reason to suppose he'd killed Willowfield, so our people checked the clothing stores. They found the fat man had bought a whole new outfit. We got a complete description of everything.'

'And then?'

'And then he disappeared. Gone. Phfffft!'

'Headed east, probably,' Henderson said. 'You'll have the hell of a job to pick his trail up if he has.'

'That's what's bothering me,' Angel said, softly. 'He laid such a dead easy trail for us to pick up as far as Council Bluffs. Then suddenly he vanishes. If he wanted to vanish, why leave a trail at all? If he didn't give a damn, how come the trail runs out?'

'Beats me,' Henderson admitted. *When the fox runs, he will always lead away from his den. You have to let him run until he believes he is no longer pursued. Then, and only then, will you see him turn for home. Then, and not before, can you take him.*

All at once he knew what to do, playing his hunch boldly, strong with the certainty of it. He had special instructions issued to all Union Pacific personnel working the transcontinental route anywhere between Kansas City and Sacramento, California, and a very special one given to every conductor: that there was a reward of $1,000 to the man who spotted the fat man and telegraphed the information to him in care of the U.S. marshal at Denver, Colorado.

It had been that simple: the one man who saw every passenger on every train moving across the rails of America was the train's conductor. Armed with information about Willowfield's clothes, his appearance, it would be a shortsighted man indeed who could not spot the fat man, and Geoffrey Marshall was certainly not that. He nailed Willowfield the first time he went through the train, and when the Transcontinental stopped at Grand Island, he ran to the telegrapher with his news.

Ten minutes later, Frank Angel and John Henderson were at the depot in Denver, stamping their feet impatiently as the engineer got steam up on the special loco that was going to run them up to Cheyenne to intercept the UP train.

'It was that simple,' Angel said.

'I see,' Willowfield said, slowly, softly, like a man afraid to let out the words. 'Alas, Mr Angel. I fear I badly underestimated you. I shall not do so again.'

'You aren't likely to get the chance,' Angel said. 'We're puffing in to Cheyenne.'

Willowfield's face was ashen, and there was a faint greasy sheen of unhealthy sweat on his forehead and upper lip. His eyes were those of a hunted animal and he jumped when Angel spoke.

'What?' he said. 'I beg your pardon, sir. What did you say?'

'I said would you like to hand over the Declaration of Independence now?'

Willowfield drew in a deep, deep breath. His gross body hardened, and something like decision came into the hunted eyes.

'Of course, sir,' he said. 'How stupid of me.'

He reached for his inside pocket in the most natural way in the world and with the Deringer he whipped from beneath his arm he shot Frank Angel point blank in the body. The heavy slug smashed Angel back against the seat and his eyes went up in his head showing only the white. Willowfield, with a surprisingly fast movement for a man so gross, rose from his seat, and in one movement of his huge arm, smashed the conductor across the carriage. A man leaped to his feet opposite, and a woman screamed as he tried to stop Willowfield, who was lurching toward the door. Snatching up the fallen carpetbag, Willowfield fended off the passenger as if he had been a small child, and wrenched open the door of the Pullman coach, stepping out on to the platform at the rear. The eddying gunsmoke whipped through after him as he swung down from the rapidly slowing train and jumped from the platform to the ground. He almost spilled over, but regained his balance, looking wildly about him for direction. He saw the scattered outbuildings of the lumber company behind the depot, and outside them, tethered horses. He started to run toward them and had gone perhaps twenty paces when he heard his name shouted.

Caution was gone now, everything gone. The buildings were so tantalizingly close, the horses so near. He ignored the shout and kept running, running to escape, and he went to hell still thinking he was going to make it.

Frank Angel, blossoming blood high on the right-hand

side of his body, had staggered off the halted train and was standing, his sixgun held in a rigidly leveled right hand clasped in turn around the wrist by his left. In this viselike grip the gun was as steady as he could hold it, and he tried very hard to hit Willowfield below the thigh, to bring him down like a running animal but not to kill him. But Frank Angel was already in shock and his hand was unsteady. The two bullets he fired fast one after the other hit George Willowfield just above the base of the spine, and the fat man went down face forward in the soft wet earth, dead before the huge body had ceased quivering.

Frank Angel holstered his sixgun and started out toward the fallen renegade. He made it exactly ten steps before he, too, fell.

FIFTEEN

The attorney general looked out at Pennsylvania Avenue.

The wide, muddy thoroughfare was packed with traffic: carriages, wagons, horsemen riding through the November drizzle, their faces like wads of dough beneath the flaring lamps. The Justice Department building was at the corner of Tenth Street, his own office on the first floor. It was a big, square room with high ceilings and French windows which opened on to an imitation balcony, unmistakably a man's room and a working room. The bookshelves were crammed with books, some lying flat, others face forward, jumbled every which way but tidy. There were law books and books on criminology, natural history, sociology, criminal jurisprudence, psychology and rehabilitation, none of them new, all of them often used for what they were, containers of information necessary to the work of the man whose office it was – the man who had prosecuted the unfortunate Andrew Johnson and secured his impeachment, and had become the chief legal adviser to the President of the United States of America.

He turned as the door to the office was opened, and his personal private secretary came in from the ante-room.

She was a tall, lissom girl with wide blue eyes and honey blonde hair tied back with a bright red ribbon. She wore a white silk blouse and a long black skirt and she had a smile like a desert sunrise. The attorney general, who was a most happily married man, was nevertheless somewhat gratified to hear that in the Justice building, Miss Rowe was sometimes referred to as 'the fair Miss Hard to Get.'

'Yes, Amabel?' he said.

'Mr Angel is here, sir,' she told him. 'Shall I send him in?'

The attorney general nodded and she stood back against the door as Frank Angel came in. He looked drawn and the deep tan on his skin looked yellowish. There were dark circles beneath his eyes, and his clothes seemed to be hanging loosely on his tall frame.

'Frank,' the attorney general said. 'Good to see you up and about. How are you feeling?'

'Pretty lousy, sir,' Angel said.

'You look like it,' his chief replied. 'Chest healing?'

'Sir,' Angel confirmed. He moved over to the leather armchair opposite the attorney general's desk, and sat down in it, lowering himself down like an old man who has been to the edge of the grave, peered in, and drawn back sharply – which, in truth was what Frank Angel had done. It was only by the merest chance that the army escort which had come to Cheyenne to take George Willowfield off the train had brought an ambulance, the still unlikelier chance that when they had rushed the severely wounded Angel across country to Fort Laramie he had arrived there in time to be treated by the surgeon general of the United States army himself. He was on an inspection tour of the Department of the Platte, Military Division of the Missouri, and he had his beautifully cut uniform off and his instruments unpacked in ten minutes flat. The operation to remove the bullet from Frank Angel's lung had been successful – a rarity in Army operations, most of which were conducted with the most primitive instruments and usually in the field – and he had been sent back east by train to convalesce. It had been a slow process. The deadly little Deringer bullet had bored through Angel's chest, burned its way through his right lung, glanced upward off a rib and fractured the scapula, lodging against that blade of bone. The surgeon general cursed even harder than he had done when he first saw Frank Angel's chest and was informed that the long, raw burn of puckered flesh on the unconscious man's back was an earlier wound and not the one he was supposed to treat.

In his report he complained bitterly at the demands that were made by 'certain departments in government' upon their men. A copy of his report had been forwarded to the attorney general, and he had made his usual notation upon it: F&F. File and forget. Amabel Rowe had filed quite a few such reports in her day.

'How was Charleston?' the attorney general asked. Angel had spent his convalescence there. It was a pretty little place and Angel said so. Then there was a silence. Neither man really wanted to bring up the subject; both knew it was unavoidable. Finally, Angel took the plunge.

'About Willowfield,' he said. The attorney general didn't say anything, just looked up expectantly.

'I tried to take him alive,' Angel said.

'I know it,' the attorney general said. 'I also know that you let friend Willowfield pull a concealed weapon on you.'

'That's right.'

'With which he then proceeded to blow a large hole in you.'

'Right.'

'Goddammit, Angel!' the attorney general exploded. 'You could be damned well dead!'

Angel grinned. He knew that the Old Man's exasperation rose out of concern for his people; he also knew exactly how well Bob Little's wife's future had been taken care of, even though the attorney general had done his best to keep it a secret.

'If it'll make you any happier, I'll go out and get run over by a dray,' he offered.

'Bah!' the attorney general snapped. 'You're so damned lucky you'd have to pay to catch bubonic plague!'

There wasn't any good answer to that, so Angel remained silent, while the attorney general reached for a cigar from the humidor on his desk.

Remembering his manners, the Old Man offered one to Angel, who shook his head hastily. The last time he had smoked one of those things, he had lost his sense of taste for three days.

'When's your leave up?' the attorney general asked, puffing at the stogie with a relish that appalled Angel.

'Already,' Angel said. 'I report back next Monday.'

'Mmm,' said the attorney general, noncommittally. 'And meanwhile? Got any plans?'

'One or two things I want to do,' Angel said. He did not elaborate. In fact, he'd already arranged to take Amabel Rowe out to dinner at a new French restaurant that had opened up in Georgetown, but telling the attorney general that would have been like touching a match to a stick of dynamite: the Old Man was notoriously protective of the beautiful Amabel. Angel changed the subject with a question.

'Falco and Kuden?' the attorney general said. 'They were hanged at Leavenworth on the first of the month.' He gave Angel an up-from-under look. 'Two out of the whole gang. Not much use my giving you orders to capture, not kill, is it?'

'Not when they can shoot back, sir,' Angel said.

'Your humor's getting worse than your reflexes,' the attorney general said gruffly. 'Go on, go on, get yourself out of here. I've got a lot of problems besides you!'

Angel grinned, getting up to leave. The Old Man never changed: his bite was worse than his bark. He felt better already.

'Those plans of yours,' the attorney general said, as Angel opened the door to the anteroom.

'Sir?'

'They don't by any chance include a, ah, young lady, do they?'

'Well, as a matter of fact they do, sir,' Angel said, tentatively.

'Oh, wonderful, wonderful,' said the attorney general, rising from his chair and coming across the room. He thrust two pieces of pasteboard into Frank Angel's hand, a broad smile spreading across his face.

'Wife and I can't use these,' he said. 'So you take them. Take your young lady. She'll enjoy it. You'll both enjoy it.'

'Well, thank you, sir,' Angel said, taking the tickets. 'What are they for?' Amabel Rowe was watching expectantly from her desk, a suppressed smile pressing a dimple into her right cheek.

'What for?' the attorney general said. 'Why – to see the Freedom Train! What else?'

He looked at Angel and Angel looked at him and then they started to grin and then the laughter came and then they were howling with laughter, roaring with it. After a little while, Amabel Rowe joined in.

It looked like it might be a halfway decent Christmas.